THE QUEST CONTINUES

Adapted by Kay Woodward from a story
created by CBBC Scotland and Brian Ward

CHAPTER ONE

The Magic
is Awakened

It was nearly time to go. Marnie McBride had waited for this moment for months, but now it had finally come, she was gripped with a sudden reluctance – because leaving Edinburgh also meant leaving Dad.

Marnie glanced up at her father, who looked as uncomfortable and nervous as she felt. She stepped towards him and was instantly engulfed in a great bear hug.

"Don't worry, Dad. Grandma and Gramps will take good care of me," Marnie said in a muffled voice. "And you'll see me in a few weeks."

"I know, I know," he replied. "I'm – I'm just being…"

Marnie grinned bravely. "Just being Dad, right?"

He smiled and planted a kiss on top of Marnie's blonde head.

"Mr McBride?" a woman's voice interrupted.

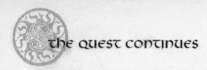

The American accent reminded Marnie sharply of home and she swung round to see a beaming young woman standing beside the check-in desk.

"And you must be Marnie," said the flight attendant brightly. "Are you ready to go?"

Marnie shrugged awkwardly and turned back to Dad, who bent down and spoke softly to her. "I love you, sweetheart," he said, hugging her once more. "Take care, OK?"

"OK," Marnie whispered. But she couldn't help thinking uneasily of the danger she knew lay ahead.

In a deserted corner of Edinburgh Airport's departure lounge, Marnie cautiously unzipped her backpack and unloaded its precious contents – the Shoebox Zoo.

There was Ailsa, a golden snake made of tiny, patterned links. Her elegant head was sleek and beautiful, with a minute forked tongue poking between sharp fangs, and eyes that glowed emerald green. Bruno the bear was made of stone, but at first glance, his chiselled coat was so realistic it looked like fur. Last of all, there was a short, squat metal eagle with odd wings: one wide, sweeping and perfectly made, the other a mishmash of scrap metal. His name was Edwin. And Edwin was *not* happy.

"We're not mere *cargo*, to be thrown in the hold willy-nilly," the eagle spluttered, pointing crossly with his wing at Marnie's boarding pass. "We expect to travel like you – in Premier Tourist Class!"

"It'sss the leassst you can do for usss after a fruitlesss Quesssst that ended up with only a copy of the Book," hissed Ailsa.

Marnie's mind whirled back to the previous year, when she'd been catapulted into the greatest adventure of her eleven years. The Quest had chosen her to find *The Book of Forbidden Knowledge*. The Book that contained the secret of life itself. The Book that, in the wrong hands, could destroy the world.

It was the Book that had once corrupted four students and caused the great wizard Michael Scot to transform them into toy creatures – an eagle, a snake, a bear and a wolf. Marnie gulped as she remembered Wolfgang, the fourth member of the Shoebox Zoo. He had tried to help Marnie complete her Quest and had paid the ultimate price.

The Book had tricked everyone, including Marnie. It had also deceived the tormented Michael Scot, his humble servant McTaggart, and Toledo, the evil Shapeshifter. For the Book that she'd found had been a fake. The real Book lay across the great ocean, in America. Only the Chosen One could find the Book and that Chosen One was Marnie McBride.

Marnie snapped back to the present and glared at Ailsa, who was flicking her tongue impatiently. "Well, we're on a *new* Quest now," Marnie reminded her. "And when we find the *real* Book, you can be human once again, OK?"

Ailsa didn't look convinced.

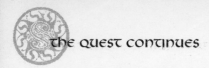

It was time for some tough talking. "Look, my twelfth birthday's not that far away," said Marnie sternly. "If you don't get a move on, then we'll never find the Book and the year will be up and you'll just have to stay toy animals forever!"

Ailsa curled away and Edwin stuck his nose in the air. Bruno shrugged, as if apologising for his friends.

Marnie sighed and decided to give in. "OK… you can go in my backpack," she said. "But you'd better behave!"

Delightedly, Edwin hopped towards the backpack as a voice blared over the loudspeaker: *"Flight 612 to Denver, Colorado, is now ready for boarding."*

Ailsa hung back. "Don't forget the torn page," she hissed. "Even a page—"

"Even a page torn from a copy of the Book may ssstill have sssecretsss to tell," mimicked Marnie. She whisked an innocent-looking magazine from her backpack, and opened it with a flourish. Tucked in the glossy sheets lay the page she'd torn from the fake Book. The intricate Native American design drawn upon the ancient paper seemed to glow.

Which is exactly what Marnie's cheeks did ten minutes later, when she was told that the Shoebox Zoo would have to travel in the cargo hold. Apparently, Edwin's pointy wing was far too dangerous to be allowed in the cabin.

"No!" cried Marnie, totally outraged. This just wasn't

4

fair. She was an eleven-year-old girl, *not* an international spy. The customs' officer and flight attendant exchanged a concerned look and Marnie suddenly realised that she might not *be* an international spy, but she was probably *acting* like one. "OK," she said, backing down quickly. The Shoebox Zoo could manage fine without her for a few hours, but there was something else she *did* want to keep with her. "I just have to get my magazine," she added, reaching for it and swiftly tucking the torn page inside. She zipped the backpack firmly shut.

"Don't worry, Marnie," the flight attendant said cheerily, patting her shoulder. "We'll make sure that your... er... animals have as smooth a ride as you do. It'll be just like they're travelling in Premier."

Briskly, the customs' officer slapped a *SECURITY – CARGO* sticker on Marnie's backpack and dumped it onto the conveyor belt. She watched nervously as it sailed away, its familiar navy and pale blue colours disappearing out of sight.

Seconds later, a backpack that was identical in every way tipped from another conveyor belt and landed right behind Marnie's hand luggage. Then they were both carried towards flight 612.

"Now, if there's anything you need, just press this buzzer here," said the ever-helpful flight attendant, after showing Marnie to her seat.

Marnie hurriedly plastered a smile to her face and

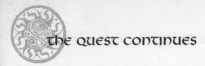

shook her head. "It's OK, I'm all right now," she said.

"Hey, don't worry," the woman chirruped. "I just saw them stow your luggage down below. Your little buddies are going to be just fine!"

As the flight attendant moved away down the aisle, Marnie settled back in her seat and tried to relax. After all, the Shoebox creatures were nine hundred years old – they could look after themselves. Before she knew it, the aircraft was thundering down the runway. It rose majestically into the sky and headed west. Towards home.

Marnie McBride wasn't the only one travelling across the great ocean. At that exact moment, a very important visitor was hauling himself wearily from a yellow taxi in front of the Fairmont Springs Hotel.

"Two hours in a taxi!" stormed Michael Scot, swirling his velvet cloak around him and brandishing his long staff. "I thought we were supposed to be staying in the city?"

The great wizard's servant nodded. "I thought the surroundings would be more to your taste, sir," McTaggart said, nervously tugging at his threadbare tartan uniform and adjusting his large, furry hat. He pointed quickly to the still blue lake nearby and the towering mountains that overlooked the hotel. "And I thought we were supposed to be keeping a low profile," he added quietly, glancing over his shoulder.

"Stop worrying!" hissed Michael. He rolled his

eyes at McTaggart's hat, before snatching it from his servant's head and flinging it to the ground. "No one knows we're here!"

But someone did. That someone had long, plaited grey hair, a craggy face and wore snakeskin cowboy boots. The Native American watched as the wizard stalked into the hotel, followed by his faithful servant.

Not a smile nor a frown crossed his old face.

Inside the Fairmont Springs Hotel, the argument went on. "You said that you wouldn't interfere," insisted McTaggart. "*The Quest continues, Marnie. You have to find the Book.* That's what you said." He stumbled after Michael Scot, his arms laden with suitcases.

The great wizard did not bother to reply, but strode onwards, further and higher into the enormous hotel. Eventually, he stopped in front of a heavy wooden door and checked the room number. It was 1111, of course. A gentle nudge and the door swung open to reveal a magnificent, wood-panelled suite of rooms, filled with antique furniture. The centrepiece was a huge, four-poster bed, hung with blood-red drapes.

"Look what happened last time you interfered," persisted McTaggart. Then his voice softened. "You lost Wolfgang, your own son."

At this, the colour drained from Michael Scot's face and he slumped weakly onto the bed.

McTaggart opened the first suitcase and stepped back in disbelief as a glittering cloud burst from it,

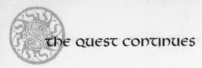

swirling wildly before metamorphosing into an ornate golden mask.

"So you think spying on the Chosen One with this daft contraption is going to help matters?" The servant's face was stiff with disapproval.

"I think you've made your point, McTaggart!" growled the great wizard, his expression dark and forbidding.

As the passenger jet rumbled through the night, Marnie slept fitfully. A mysterious breeze flipped open the pages of her magazine to reveal the torn page. Then something magical began to happen. The runes that made up the Native American design lifted from the page and swirled around to reveal a colourful, leaping horse. As the runes settled back into their original positions, the creature vanished.

Dreams chased through Marnie's mind – old dreams and new dreams...

Cloaked figures ran through the courtyard at Tantallon, one clutching a hefty leather-bound book covered with strange markings. Then the book was hidden inside a wooden barrel by another slender figure. The barrel tumbling from a cliff into the stormy sea below... A young pioneer, dressed in furs and skins, took the heavy tome from the safety of the barrel. He handed it to a Native American chief... Then a ceremony began and the chief joined the hands of the pioneer and a pretty young Native American woman. Whoosh! Toledo the

Shapeshifter rocketed upwards, in his hands a copy of The Book of Forbidden Knowledge. *He erupted spectacularly in a ball of flame.*

Marnie's eyes snapped open. She was filled with a sudden horror at the vision of Toledo. He was dead, wasn't he...? And there was something else. The pioneer of her dream had looked uncannily like her Dad. She couldn't even begin to get her head round *that.*

Marnie shivered. She hadn't suffered these nightmarish visions since she'd destroyed the fake book. So why had they suddenly returned? And what did they *mean?*

In the darkness of room 1111, Michael Scot leapt from his bed as if demons were chasing him. With a trembling finger, he pointed at the grate and a fire burst into life. Then he grasped a red-hot poker, and pointed it randomly around the shadowy room.

"Show yourself!" the great wizard demanded. "Who dares disturb the sleep of Michael Scot?"

A hand tapped him on the shoulder and Michael swung round, his face a mask of terror.

It was McTaggart. "You've been dreaming again," he said gently.

His calming words made no difference to the delirious wizard. Michael Scot continued to whirl around the room, jabbing the poker into dark corners. Then abruptly he stopped, and his eyes grew wide.

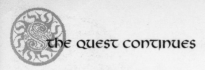

"The child is in danger!" he roared.

"Marnie?" whispered McTaggart. "What kind of danger?"

But Michael Scot was spent, and his head sagged low on defeated shoulders. Slowly, his servant helped him back to bed.

CHAPTER TWO

OUT OF
THE WATER...

Tired beyond belief, Marnie pushed her laden trolley, with her backpack perched safely on top, through the arrivals gate at Denver International Airport. Then she felt tears rush into her eyes. There they were, the two familiar faces that she'd missed so much.

"Gramps!" she called. "Grandma!"

Her grandparents rushed forward to gather her into their waiting arms. It had been almost a year since she'd seen them, but they'd hardly changed. There was Gramps, with his dark hair, brown eyes and wide smile, and her silvery-blonde Grandma, whose twinkling grey eyes could make anyone feel welcome, especially a granddaughter who'd flown from Scotland to visit.

"Take care, Marnie," trilled the flight attendant, as she waved goodbye.

"Thanks!" called Marnie, before hurrying in her

11

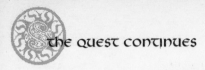

grandparents' wake through the busy terminal.

And then she saw him. In the middle of an otherwise deserted row of plastic seats was a Native American man as old as her grandfather. His long, grey hair was plaited, his clothes straight from the set of a Western, and on his feet were a pair of snakeskin cowboy boots. He sat motionless, apart from his dark, piercing eyes, which followed Marnie as she walked past. The man's eyes flicked quickly towards her backpack, which she grasped involuntarily.

Marnie broke his gaze for just a second, to steer around a pile of luggage. When she looked back, he was gone.

The late afternoon sun was casting shadows on newly mown grass as Gramps' station wagon cruised to a halt. Marnie peered out at the beautifully kept cemetery. This was the moment she'd wished for and dreaded in equal measure. Apprehensively, she climbed out of the vehicle, a bunch of brightly coloured flowers clutched tightly in her hand.

Grandma and Gramps came after her, but Marnie stopped them. "It's OK," she said. "I'll be all right on my own."

Marnie walked slowly towards a white, marble headstone, then crouched before it. The inscription read simply:

Rosemary McBride
Loving Wife
Mother
Daughter

Placing her flowers at the base of the headstone, she began to speak softly, sadly. "I really miss you, Mom, especially with all this Quest stuff going on..." She hesitated, then decided to plough on. "And what about my dream? What's a guy who looks like Dad doing with a bunch of Native Americans? Is he some kind of ancestor or something?"

She paused. For a moment, she almost felt like her mom would reply. She felt so *near*, so close to her... But the moment passed and the familiar feeling of loss returned. "Maybe it's just a dream," Marnie whispered. "Not everything has to be magic, right?" She hung her head, unsure how to explain her feelings. "It's–it's good to talk to you, but I kind of need someone who's, you know... here. And I can't talk to Gramps and Grandma because this stuff would totally freak them out." An idea popped into her head. "Maybe I should talk to Kyle...? I have to talk to *somebody*."

She looked back to see Grandma wringing her hands. "I have to go," Marnie said hurriedly. "I really miss you, Mom... I wish you were here." She kissed her fingertips, placed them lightly on the headstone and took a deep, shuddering breath. Then she headed back to her anxious grandparents.

Just twenty minutes later, they pulled up in front

of a sprawling, mustard clapperboard house. Marnie couldn't help smiling as she recognised Gramps and Grandma's home.

Then she spotted a lone figure kicking a hacky-sack on the drive. "Kyle!" she yelled, jumping out of the station wagon and throwing her arms around the Native American boy. "Hey, I didn't know you were coming! I've got *so* much to tell you about Scotland."

Kyle gave an embarrassed grin. "Yeah, well… I was just, you know… passing through." He nodded hello to Marnie's grandparents.

"Hi, Kyle," said Grandma. "Do you want to stay for supper? It's my home-made meatloaf."

It was an offer that Kyle couldn't refuse. A few hours later, after two helpings of meatloaf and a slice of cake, he followed Marnie upstairs to her room. "So, what's the big deal?" he asked, leaning against the wall. "Did you see the Loch Ness Monster or something?"

Marnie held onto her backpack tightly. "You have to swear first," she warned. "Swear that you won't tell anybody."

"Don't you trust me?" asked Kyle. He gave a nervous laugh.

"Yeah, I trust you," said Marnie patiently. "But this is, like, really important."

"OK, I swear," said Kyle.

Marnie looked at the photo of her mother. It was the very first thing she'd unpacked and her most treasured possession. "Swear on the memory of my mom," she insisted.

Kyle hesitated, then relented. "I swear on the memory of your mom."

Marnie nodded solemnly and gathered her thoughts. She couldn't deal with this secret alone any longer. It was time. "Right. Inside this bag, there's an eagle, a snake and a bear…"

She took a deep breath and thrust her hand inside the backpack and knew instantly that something was wrong. In dismay, she pulled out a kilted teddy bear. She didn't dare look at Kyle who was sure to think she was crazy by now. Instead, she plunged her hand back inside the backpack and rummaged around desperately. But it was no use.

"This is somebody else's bag," she groaned. "*Somebody else has got the Shoebox Zoo!*"

The Shoebox creatures were starting to feel slightly sick. Every time the backpack travelled round a bend, they were thrown to one side. And they were going round an awful lot of bends.

"Wh–wh–what can you see, Edwin?" Bruno asked the little eagle, who was doing his best to unzip the backpack from the inside.

"I can't see anything if you insist on getting in the way, you great lummox!" puffed Edwin.

"Why don't you both get out of the way and let me take a look?" Ailsa said briskly, poking an emerald eye to the tiny gap. But within seconds, she'd slithered

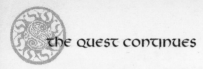

to the far side of the backpack.

Bruno and Edwin exchanged worried glances.

"There'sss a monsssster out there!" Ailsa hissed in terror. "It'sss asss big asss a houssse!" Then she froze. "I can hear footsssstepsss!"

A Native American man with long, grey plaited hair and snakeskin cowboy boots plucked the backpack from the luggage carousel, where it had been travelling round and round. He carried it over to the display of fierce, papier mâché animals that loomed over the carousel. Here, he unzipped the backpack and peered inside.

"Arrrrrgggggghhhhh!" howled Edwin, Ailsa and Bruno in unison.

"Hey, keep the volume down," said the man, his words slow and deliberate. "I've been waiting for you a long, long time."

Bruno raised an eyebrow and peered at the others. They looked as confused as he did.

"Now, you lie still and be real quiet, OK?" their captor said. "Or maybe I'll just feed you to these guys." He turned the backpack opening towards the mighty paper mâché hippopotamus. The Shoebox Zoo shrank back in horror from the terrible monster and watched helplessly as their escape route was swiftly zipped shut.

Gramps put the phone down and turned to face Marnie. "Well, there's been some kind of mix-up," he said. "But they think they'll have found your bag by the morning, OK, honey?" Gramps patted her shoulder reassuringly.

It was no good. Marnie felt sick to the pit of her stomach. What if she never found the Shoebox Zoo? Without her, they had no chance of *ever* becoming human again!

"Hey, they'll turn up," said Kyle, picking up his basketball.

Marnie's words could barely be heard. "I guess you'll never believe me now, huh?" she murmured.

Kyle gave a helpless shrug. "Night, Marnie," he said. "See you tomorrow."

It was late — the hands on the bedside clock were edging closer and closer to eleven o'clock. Marnie McBride was trying to use her power to summon the Shoebox Zoo. She sat cross-legged on her bed, her arms stretched wide and her eyes tightly shut.

"Come to me. I command you," she muttered, concentrating so hard that she could feel the blood pulsing through her temples. "*I command you to come to me!*"

Nothing.

Marnie's arms flopped miserably onto the bed. "Come on, you guys. Where *are* you?" she pleaded.

Still nothing. Marnie stifled a yawn and decided to watch television instead. She zapped the remote control and a woman with curly red hair appeared on the screen. She wore so many different types of fabric that she looked as if she'd robbed a curtain store. Perched on her head was a strange cloth hat hung with shiny crystals. Before her was a crystal ball and a pack of cards.

"… joining me on another journey down life's strange highway," the woman was saying. "Through me, a grieving mother has spoken with her dearly departed child. A long-lost twin has been reunited with his earthbound brother."

She spoke in a melodic way that was almost hypnotic. Marnie's eyelids grew heavy and she felt herself drawn in by the psychic's ramblings, tempted by the irresistible thought that here was one way she could speak to Mom again.

"We have marvelled at the marvellous, known the unknowable and returned to our humble living rooms safe and sound," continued the woman. "So, it's good-bye until the next time, when Aurora Dexter takes you *Above and Beyond*!"

But Marnie didn't hear the final words. She was asleep.

In a dingy television studio on the other side of town, Aurora Dexter ripped off her microphone and hurried from the set.

"Way to go, Aurora!" shouted the camera operator after her. "You almost had *me* convinced there."

"Local cable TV," the psychic muttered, as she stomped over to the poky corner that masqueraded as her dressing room. She sat down and stared at her reflection in a mirror framed with dim lightbulbs. "Face facts, Aurora," she said firmly. "Unless you can get yourself on Channel 411, you might as we'll pack your bags and head on home to Valentine, Nebraska."

With a wry smile, she reached out for her pack of cards. "Let's just see what destiny has in store for tomorrow," she murmured, dividing the pack into four. Slowly, she turned over the top card from each pile. First, the Jack of Hearts, then the Jack of Clubs, finally, two more Jacks. Four cards – each worth eleven. The psychic frowned, then shrugged.

The clock above her mirror struck eleven...

...at the same time as Marnie McBride's alarm went off...

...and Michael Scot's ancient clock struck.

The last chime echoed through the darkened hotel room. Then there was an ominous silence.

"It has struck again," murmured the great wizard fearfully, "for only the second time in eleven hundred years." His lips barely moved as he breathed the final, dreadful words. "The second prophecy..."

McTaggart gasped in horror.

Michael took a great, shuddering gulp of air, then strode across the room. "Give me the eyes!" he commanded, placing his hand on the golden mask. The mask shook and beams of light poured from between the ornate panels. Instantly, the wizard was racing across jagged mountaintops, then swooping down over a wide lake. In the distance, the turquoise water began to bubble then a tall figure in white broke the surface, rising majestically above the lake. His face wore a look of terrible vengeance.

"Toledo!" cried Michael Scot.

"How *can* it be him?" McTaggart asked frantically. "It's impossible! He's *dead*, isn't he? Wh—"

"Will you stop your infernal chattering and let me *think!*" roared his master. He drew a long, slow breath and, when he spoke, his words seemed to come from far away and long ago…

In every generation dawns a most auspicious day,

The day when four elevens meet and Sleepers have their say,

The day to which the fickle sands of time and tide have run,

The day when fate and prophecy reveal the Chosen One…"

This prophecy had predicted Marnie's original Quest for *The Book of Forbidden Knowledge*. Now, there was more.

"But when the clock does chime again, and hours and minutes pass,

The cogs will turn relentlessly behind the cloudy glass,

Until the Dawn Queen's faithless hand shall open up the Book,

Then death and darkness will descend on all who dare to look..."

"So what does it all mean?" asked McTaggart hesitantly. "What does this have to do with Toledo?"

Michael's next words were laced with dread. "Into the water was he cast, and out of the water shall he return."

A menacing laugh echoed around the hotel. It came from the lake.

Marnie McBride sat bolt upright in bed, her breathing ragged, her eyes wide with shock. Something terrible had happened, she just knew it. But *what*?

CHAPTER THREE

The BALANCE OF POWER

By the time sunlight had begun to glow through her bedroom curtains, Marnie had decided that her troubled sleep wasn't worth worrying about. This sort of thing happened with jetlag, right? No, she was more concerned about the whereabouts of the Shoebox Zoo. They'd been lost before, but never for this long. And what about Kyle? Would he ever believe her enough to help with the Quest? Totally dejected, she trudged downstairs.

To Marnie's surprise, Kyle was sitting at the table, as comfortable as if this was *his* house. Before she could speak, Gramps burst out of the kitchen, carrying two stacks of pancakes that were oozing with glossy maple syrup. He plonked the plates on to the table and Marnie slid onto her seat. Boy, was she hungry.

"So, what do you think about me mixing in the world of showbiz?" Gramps chuckled, twirling round to reveal the 'Security' logo on the back of his shirt. "Not everybody's grandpa works for a TV star!"

"I'd hardly call Aurora Dexter a TV star," called Grandma from the kitchen.

"Aurora Dexter?" Marnie mumbled, her mouth packed with pancake.

"Sure," said Kyle. "You know, Becky's mom."

Marnie was beginning to get the feeling that she'd been away from Denver for years, not months. "Becky from our class?" she asked. "Her mom is that cheesy woman who talks to dead people on TV?"

"I sent you an e-mail all about it," said Kyle shortly. "If you'd bothered to get back to me—"

"I was kind of busy!" snapped Marnie.

Gramps jumped in hurriedly. "Well, I'm taking you guys over there this afternoon, OK?" He sidled into the kitchen to talk to Grandma.

There was an awkward silence.

"Did your Shoebox Zoo show up yet?" asked Kyle casually.

Marnie glared at him. "What do *you* care?" she said. "You don't believe in them. You don't believe *anything* that I told you."

Kyle gave her a blank look. Then he reached under the table and pulled out a navy backpack with light blue panels. "Abracadabra!" he announced proudly. "I just found this on the porch."

Hardly daring to hope, Marnie unzipped the backpack and her heart lifted. They were back!

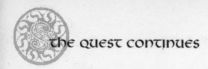

"Wow," said Kyle. "They're *old*."

"Shhh, they'll hear you," whispered Marnie, gazing at her beloved Shoebox creatures that were perched on her bed. Edwin stood with his wings outstretched proudly, Bruno was ready to pounce and Ailsa was curled into a neat coil. They were totally still. "Come on, you guys. Where have you been?" she asked eagerly.

They didn't move.

Kyle snorted with laughter.

Marnie felt her euphoria begin to seep away. Had something dreadful happened to the Shoebox Zoo while they'd been out of her sight? She tried the words she'd once used to wake them. "Awake, awake, for I am your master!"

Nothing.

Kyle picked up Ailsa and examined her closely. "You know, I nearly bought into this whole crazy story," he said, looking the little snake right in the eye. "I mean, they're really cool, but wizards and castles and talking statues and stuff—"

He broke off suddenly. A tiny humming noise was weaving mysteriously around the room. It was coming from Ailsa.

Marnie sighed with relief. She looked at Kyle and tried not to giggle at his horrified expression.

"OK," said Kyle nervously. "Where do the batteries go?"

Suddenly, the snake began to writhe in his grasp.

"Got you!" she hissed.

The colour drained from Kyle's face, and he flung Ailsa away. She landed neatly beside Edwin and Bruno, who were performing a quick jig on the duvet.

"Seeing is believing!" shouted Edwin gaily.

Marnie beamed. Kyle *had* to believe her now. "Are you OK?" she asked quietly. "Because I know they're kind of scary if you're not ready for them."

"Scared? Me?" said Kyle, his voice wobbly. "I wasn't scared, no way."

"My humble apologiesss," hissed Ailsa, bowing her beautiful head.

"Ahem," coughed Edwin politely. "Delighted to meet you, young fellow." He hopped towards Kyle and held out his good wing.

Kyle backed further away. "This is *way* too weird," he mumbled.

"Boo!" growled Bruno. Then he hung his head. "Sorry, Kyle," mumbled the friendliest member of the Shoebox Zoo.

"So… who, I mean, *what*, are you?" said Kyle hesitantly. He looked *very* uncomfortable.

Edwin waved his wings imperiously. "That, my young friend, is a long story. A long, long, long story…" He puffed out his chest proudly ready to embark on a long story, when Bruno butted in.

"We were students of the wizard, Michael Scot, right?" the bear said quickly. "And, er, we stole his book of magic, so he turned us into these, er…

25

animals and now we've got to help Marnie – she's the Chosen One – to get the book back so that we can be human again." It was probably the longest speech he'd ever made, but was still several hours shorter than Edwin's version of events.

Now it was Ailsa's turn. "Only there were four of usss," she said sadly. "Wolfgang – a noble wolf and ssson of the great Michael Ssscot – died to sssave usss… and to keep Toledo the Ssshapessshifter from getting the book."

Edwin ruffled his feathers. "Yes, well, that just about sums it up, I suppose," he said.

Kyle gulped. "So, you're real people?" he asked in a small voice. "You're just trapped in these shapes by… magic?"

"Everything I've told you is true," said Marnie earnestly. "The Shoebox Zoo is real. Michael Scot is real. And the Quest is real too."

By now, Kyle looked utterly shell-shocked. Marnie felt a rush of sympathy for him and remembered how she'd once rejected everything to do with the Quest. She hadn't wanted to be involved, not one bit. So perhaps Kyle could do with a couple of hours off…

"Look, why don't I meet you later?" she suggested. "Then we can go to the studio with Gramps."

Kyle nodded and was out of the door faster than Marnie could say *Toledo the Shapeshifter*. He'd obviously had more than enough magic for one day. As for the Chosen One, she was just getting started...

"The torn page!" she exclaimed, grabbing her magazine and fanning the pages until she found what she was looking for. Edwin stumbled backwards in the sudden breeze.

Marnie spread the ancient page on her lap and examined the symbols, her eyes tracing the outline of the circular pattern and flicking to and fro between the colourful feathers. She stared. And stared. And absolutely *nothing* happened.

"Perhaps the torn page works its own magic?" said Bruno wisely. "Perhaps you can't will it, Mistress."

"Well, why is it that I don't seem to have any power any more?" asked Marnie helplessly. In Scotland, she'd been bubbling over with weird magic, but now there was nothing. Not a trickle.

Edwin rubbed his beak thoughtfully. "Well, if you ask *me*," he said, "it's all to do with the positive and the negative — what we early scientists would call the balance of power." For once, he had everyone's attention. Edwin liked nothing better than an audience. "If your power is positive," he said to Marnie, "then it must somehow be being countered by an equal negative force."

This didn't make sense to Marnie. A negative force ... from where? Toledo was dead, she'd seen that with her own eyes. "Positive and negative..." she said, thinking aloud. "Good and evil... That's the balance of everything, right? Even the Book..." Marnie had the feeling that she was on the verge of something big. "What if the negative force is coming from the Book or something?" she suggested.

Edwin was now hopping from one foot to the other with excitement. "Which means that it might be very close!" he squeaked.

Marnie looked again at the torn page. "There have to be clues," she said quietly. "That's the whole thing about the Quest — a whole bunch of clues that fit together to help lead us to the Book, right?"

She frowned, trying hard to think of a single thing that might help. Then it came to her. "What about my dream on the plane?" The Native American design began to glow spectacularly and Marnie was plunged again into the dizzying vision.

The young pioneer unwrapped The Book of Forbidden Knowledge... *A mysterious woman in white spun through the air... The Book was passed from hand to hand... The marriage ceremony between the pioneer and the young Native American woman took place... The white-clad woman plucked the Book from the air.*

Marnie opened her eyes wide with fear. "Somebody else wants the Book!" she gasped.

"How can this be, Master?" moaned McTaggart, his words echoing dolefully through the gloomy hotel room. "Why isn't he dead?"

Michael Scot's reply was devoid of emotion, as if he were in shock. "Toledo is empty," he said. "He is seeking power. That's why he comes to me." He reached for the golden mask, but McTaggart dragged him away.

"No, Master!" he pleaded. "It's madness!"

"What would you have me do?" the wizard bellowed. "Skulk in the shadows until he comes after me?" He lunged towards the golden mask, which burst into life, sending shards of light shooting through the hotel room.

At once, the great wizard could see the glowing figure rising from the churning waters of the lake. "Go back!" Michael shouted. "Go back through the fire and the watery hole to where you belong *and do not return*!"

Toledo hovered above the lake – a wispy, insubstantial spectre whose dark eyes throbbed with hatred. "Have you forgotten so soon, old man?" he taunted. "My power is *your* power, remember? At last, I have come to claim it, the greatest power of all. *The power of the Book*!"

"You shall not have it!" roared Michael Scot, clamping his hand more firmly to the mask.

At once, a great beam of fizzing, crackling light leapt from Toledo's fingertips and arched high into the air, travelling from the lake to the Fairmont Springs Hotel, where it curved down again, heading towards Room 1111. It made contact with the golden mask, greedily sucking energy from the great wizard. And as Michael Scot weakened, Toledo grew stronger

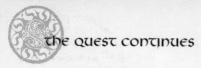
and stronger.

The Shapeshifter gave a great, blood-curdling yell – and it was over. "For now, you shall see no more of me," he cried, vanishing from sight. His evil laugh echoed around the mountains as the great wizard slumped to the floor.

CHAPTER FOUR

BEYOND THE GRAVE

In her dingy dressing room at the Starbeam TV studios, Aurora Dexter was trying her best to make contact with the spirits. She wasn't finding it easy.

"Speak!" she wailed dramatically, her palms stretched towards the ceiling. "Speak to me! Is there anybody there?"

There was a gentle tapping noise and Aurora stiffened expectantly. But as Gramps poked his friendly face around the doorway, her shoulders sagged.

"I don't mean to butt in..." he said softly, "but this is my granddaughter, Marnie, and her buddy, Kyle."

Aurora's eyes rested briefly on Marnie, before widening with delight as she looked past her. "Kyle!" she exclaimed. "Becky's told me so much about you. Come in!"

Kyle swayed uncomfortably from foot to foot, while Marnie raised an eyebrow at the rapturous welcome he'd received. She rested her backpack against a pile of dusty old books and scanned the messy room. Cables snaked across the floor and television studio equipment was scattered everywhere. On the far side of the room was a tiny stage, with a battered, old film camera poised in front of it. So this was the glitzy world of television, was it? She was seriously unimpressed.

"Is it all right if they sit in on the recording?" asked Gramps.

"Oh, sure," said Aurora, glancing around her and looking glum. Then her dark eyes began to sparkle. "Of course, when I do the show for Channel 411, I'll have a *real* audience and a bigger studio."

Gramps was fidgeting and looked uncomfortable. "Anyway... don't be a bother to Aurora," he said to Marnie and Kyle. "See you later!"

The door had barely swung shut behind Gramps when Aurora pointed a scarlet-tipped finger at Kyle. "Let me guess, I'm *never* wrong," she murmured, rising from her chair and moving towards Marnie's friend. "Sagittarius!" she announced proudly.

Kyle nodded slowly.

The psychic rose and walked to Marnie, circling her slowly, almost menacingly. Marnie started to feel uneasy, even though she knew that the woman must be a fraud. Anyone could pretend to speak with the dead, right?

But Aurora was putting on a good show. "No," she

whispered in disbelief. "We can't really share the same birthday, can we? Scorpio. The eleventh day of the eleventh month?"

Despite herself, Marnie was now feeling distinctly uncomfortable. Aurora must have used some kind of trick to work out her birthday, but why would she pretend that they were both born on the same day? The day when four elevens meet…

Bang! The door rattled on its hinges as a girl Marnie's age barged into the room and the tension was shattered. "Hi, Kyle," the girl said in a singsong voice, draping her arm around his shoulders.

"Yeah, hi," mumbled Kyle.

It was Aurora's daughter, Becky. To say that she and Marnie had never hit it off would have been putting it mildly – they were the best of enemies.

"Hi," interrupted Marnie, when it became obvious that Becky only had eyes for Kyle.

Becky turned to her with a look of disdain. "Marnie," she said flatly. "Welcome back. How was Ireland?"

Marnie grimaced. Yep, still the same old Becky. "Scotland, actually," she said.

"Whatever." Becky shrugged her shoulders. Then her voice became as breezy as an autumn day. "Hey, Kyle. I'm going to hit the mall. Want to come?"

Kyle glanced awkwardly at Marnie. "Well, we're here for the show, actually," he said.

"Becky, honey," Aurora began, seemingly unaware

of the tense atmosphere. "If you're going to the mall, take care. Have you got your crystal?"

"I'm wearing my crystal, Mom," groaned Becky. She lifted her pendant. "See? No harm can come to me."

Aurora gave her daughter an affectionate smile. "Be back soon, you hear?"

"Sure," nodded Becky, rolling her eyes. "Are you coming, Kyle?"

"Er, not right now," muttered Kyle, who now looked as if he'd rather be swimming with killer whales than standing between Becky and Marnie.

"OK!" sang Becky, and – *mwah!* – she planted another kiss on Kyle's reluctant cheek. "Bye, Marnie. Good to see you," she drawled, before walking jauntily towards the door and aiming a deft kick at the backpack. It fell open, sending a surprised-looking Bruno skittering across the floor.

"Oops," said Becky casually.

"Let me see that," the psychic said, eagerly reaching for Bruno.

But Marnie was faster, her fingers closing tightly around the little bear. She couldn't have explained why, but she knew that she didn't want Becky's mom touching Bruno.

"Bye, Mom," shouted an irritated Becky from the doorway. "I'm leaving now."

The star of Starbeam TV tore her gaze away from the little bear and hurried after her daughter. "Honey, while you're out, will you pick up some more incense for me?" she called. Becky rolled her eyes. "Anything but patchouli. The spirits can't abide patchouli…"

Marnie heaved a sigh of relief. "That was a close call," she whispered to Kyle.

"Hey, don't worry about her," said Kyle under his breath. "She's just a big phoney."

"Which one?" asked Marnie. As far as she was concerned, both Becky and her mother were total fakes.

It wasn't long before the cameras were rolling and, no matter how sceptical Marnie felt, she found herself enjoying the show. Aurora had put several callers in touch with their loved ones, including Lucille from Cheyenne Wells, Colorado, who was convinced that her uncle had buried jewels in the garden before his death. Unfortunately, the spirits didn't give an exact location of the treasure, but Aurora told Lucille that her uncle sent his love.

"Ah…" the psychic continued mysteriously, "I have another dear one who wants to come through. Yes, I want to send a message to… Mary? No, no, not Mary. Mandy? Starting with Ma… The spirits aren't speaking very clearly." She raised her voice. "Speak more clearly, spirits!"

"Maybe it's for Marnie?" Kyle chuckled quietly.

Marnie smiled uncertainly. She was starting to get a weird feeling about this.

"Is there a little girl who's lost a pet dog?" Aurora's

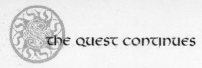

voice was trembling now.

"A dog?" asked Lucille, who was still on the line.

"A dog with a German name," said Aurora, her eyelids flickering. Another great spasm ran through her body. "Wilhelm or Wilf or Wulfric... Was he lost in a fire?"

This was too close to the truth for Marnie. With a jolt, she remembered how the Shapeshifter had fed the beautiful blue and gold wolf to the flames.

"He didn't like fire," insisted Aurora. "And his name was German..."

"His name was Buck," said Lucille. "But he was a German shepherd. What's old Buck saying?"

"No, not Buck..." Aurora now seemed strangely out of control, as if a power were taking over her body. "Wilf? Wolfie?" she continued, and at last found the name she sought. "*Wolfgang!*" With a cry of pain, she went limp.

Nothing could have prepared Marnie for this. She was powerless to do anything but stare.

"Aurora, are you OK?" called the floor manager uncertainly. "Go to commercial!"

Everyone crowded round the unconscious psychic – everyone apart from Marnie. She couldn't move. Every bone in her body felt as heavy as lead, while the air around her seemed to be tingling with energy.

She was gazing at a television monitor, mesmerised by the floor manager's efforts to wake Aurora, when the image dissolved into hissing, swirling snow.

Marnie's pulse quickened. Then, with a crackle and a splutter, flames appeared on the screen and above them, pincered cruelly between a set of blackened tongs, was Wolfgang. The tongs opened and he plummeted into the fire.

"Oh, Wolfgang!" cried Marnie, the pain of Wolfgang's loss as fresh as the dark day it had happened.

"I'm sorry I failed yoooou," howled the wolf, as the flames engulfed him.

The monitor went blank.

In the distance, thunder rumbled. Marnie stared out of her bedroom window, watching forlornly as big, fat drops of rain began to fall. Kyle and the Shoebox Zoo watched her with concerned expressions. "I don't know *what* was going on," she sighed forlornly.

"Maybe Wolfgang was trying to tell you something?" suggested Edwin gently. "A clue to help us with the Quest, perhaps?"

"Or a warning?" added Ailsa ominously.

Marnie shrugged. After watching Aurora's performance, a thought had occurred to her and now it refused to go away. She tried to explain to the others. "I got the feeling that Aurora has some kind of real power," she said, picking up the photo of her mother. "And maybe that's something we could use. I mean, without power and with Michael thousands of kilometres away in Scotland... well, we need all the help we can get, don't we?"

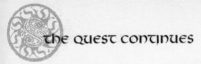

"Especially if somebody else is looking for the Book," said Bruno.

Marnie nodded. She thought for a moment – there was something she needed to know before they went any further. "Are you in, Kyle?" she asked, her eyes pleading silently with him. "Look, if we find the Book, it'll put everything right. *Everything*."

"And by the way," added Edwin, wearing his sternest expression, "if we don't find it before Marnie's twelfth birthday, the world will probably end!"

Zap! A blinding flash of lightning lit the night sky, bathing Marnie's room in an eerie glow. A split-second later, thunder crashed. The storm was almost overhead.

Kyle looked nervous – whether because of the storm or Edwin's doom-laden prediction, Marnie couldn't tell. He stumbled to his feet and started backing towards the door. "OK... I'm in," he said. "But the Quest is going to have to wait until the morning. For me, anyhow."

Before Marnie could reply, the door had clicked shut. She grinned in triumph.

Ailsa wriggled over and swayed gently in front of her. "Marnie... you're not ssseeking the Book for sssome purpossse of your own, are you?" she hissed accusingly.

Marnie started. "What purpose would that be?" she whispered, unsettled by the snake's words.

All she wanted was to put everything right, to return everything to how it once was. That was all.

Outside, Kyle sauntered down the path away from the house. He walked past a huge glistening bush, its leaves glossy with water from the rain, and headed for home. The old Native American man stepped from behind the bush and watched him go. He was wearing snakeskin cowboy boots.

McTaggart tilted a small crystal bottle over a bowl of porridge, slowly dripping tiny beads of emerald liquid onto the steamy surface. "We need you fighting fit, sir," he muttered, moving towards the silent figure in the bed. He lifted a spoonful of the healing mixture to the great wizard's lips.

But Michael Scot could not eat. "He drained the energy from me," the wizard whispered. "The balance of power has shifted... We must warn the Chosen One that the second prophecy is upon us..." His eyelids quivered shut.

"No!" The servant desperately shook his master. "Michael, tell me what must be done. I don't know what to do!"

Michael Scot's eyes struggled open. They were filled with despair. "For the first time in eleven hundred years," he said desperately, "neither do I."

CHAPTER FIVE

INSIDE THE WOODSHED

Marnie could hardly contain her excitement as the station wagon lurched down the track, through the tunnel of trees. They rounded a bend and crunched to a halt in front of the red and green, wooden house. It looked warm and inviting in the dappled sunlight. The perfect place for a summer holiday.

"Gramps!" exclaimed Marnie. She flung open the car door and dragged Kyle into the clearing. "You repainted!"

"Sure," said her grandpa. "Do you like it?"

Marnie nodded enthusiastically. This had to be her favourite place in the whole world; she'd always loved it. What made it even more special was the fact that she knew her mother had loved it too.

Grandma dragged an armful of bags from the car, among them, Marnie's backpack. She peered inside and grimaced. "I see you've brought your little friends with you," she said, giving Gramps a pointed look.

Marnie wondered briefly why Grandma was making a fuss about the Shoebox Zoo, but she didn't have time to find out. There were far more important things to do, like visiting her old haunts. "Come on, Kyle!" she said, heading for the river. He pounded after her.

It was just as she remembered it. Marnie stood on the edge, staring across the wide expanse of churning water at the far bank. Then, without warning, the scene was drained of colour…

On the far bank, there now stood a tepee. Wisps of smoke rose from it, fading quickly from sight … The Book of Forbidden Knowledge was passed from one hand to another… A solemn pact took place between the old Native American, the young woman and the pioneer, and was sealed with a clasping of hands.

It was over.

Marnie blinked as the vision cleared. She was still beside the river, but now there was no tepee, no strange agreement, no Book.

"You look like you've seen a ghost," said Kyle gently.

"One ghost?" said Marnie shakily. "Try two or three."

Kyle looked shocked. "What do you mean?" he asked.

Marnie instantly regretted her words. There was

no point worrying Kyle too. "I see stuff in my head sometimes," she explained. "It's not a big deal." But it was. And more worrying still was the realisation that these visions no longer seemed to be confined to her dreams.

"Hey, you guys!" called Gramps, his distant voice defusing the awkward atmosphere. "There's something I want to show you!"

But when she saw what the 'something' was, Marnie wished she'd stayed by the river. She warily peered into the murky, overshadowed area at the far end of her grandparents' plot of land. The trees here seemed to be taller and sturdier than elsewhere, and not a chink of light penetrated their thick foliage. But it was what lay beneath the trees that really scared her. It was the rickety old shed, its timber blackened with age, its darkened windows peering at her like evil eyes...

Marnie recoiled. "I thought you were going to tear that old shed down?" she whispered.

Gramps scratched his head. "Well, I wanted to," he explained. "But when they told me what hooking up to the power line was going to cost, I figured I'd just clean up old Ginny!"

Kyle seemed thoroughly confused. "Jenny?" he asked.

"Ginny the generator!" announced Gramps, with a chuckle. He wrenched open the doors to reveal a huge engine that squatted in the shed like an ugly, mechanical ogre. "Hey, Marnie, remember when you thought there was a ghost in here, when you were little?"

Of course Marnie remembered. How could she forget the throbbing, sputtering generator that used to terrify her? It didn't matter how many times everyone had told her that it was just a machine. To her, it was just plain spooky.

Marnie uneasily watched as Gramps reached for the start cord. "She's not going to bite," he said, with a quick yank. Nothing happened. "She just needs a little coaxing…" he muttered.

Marnie stared with growing apprehension. Then…

The Book whirled dizzyingly in the air. The Native Americans and the pioneers clasped hands together…

And then with a jolt, she was back, watching fearfully as Gramps turned a crank and, with a great clackety-clack, the generator rattled noisily into life, its two yellow dials watching her like eyes. And…

Michael Scot spun round and round, old coins covering his eyes…

Marnie gasped in horror. Visions? Malevolent machines? She felt as if something truly bad was closing in on her and in a panic, she turned on her heel and ran.

"Marnie!" called Gramps, as he and Kyle stared after her in amazement.

The deathly silence of Room 1111 of the Fairmont

Springs Hotel was broken by a sharp rapping noise. At once, McTaggart dragged his tired, bloodshot eyes away from his sleeping master, stumbled to the wooden door and flung it open.

"Who dares disturb the sleep of the great Michael Scot?" the servant shouted. He looked both left and right. But the corridor was empty. *Almost* empty.

A whistle pierced the air and McTaggart looked down. There, at his feet, stood a small creature – not a member of the Shoebox Zoo, but a wooden horse with a bristly mane and tail. It was decorated with strange, colourful markings.

"The great Michael Scot, I presume?" said the horse cheerfully.

"Er, no…" said McTaggart hesitantly. Then he seemed to remember his manners. "But what can the great wizard do for you?"

The little visitor pawed the carpet with a tiny, impatient hoof. "Invite a weary stranger in for some chow?" it suggested.

Speechlessly, McTaggart stood back as the horse trotted briskly into Room 1111. There, the great wizard had awoken and weakly propped himself up on one elbow. "Would you be kind enough to tell us just who you are and what you're doing here?" he asked, his voice as feeble as that of an old man, which was exactly how he now looked.

With a leap that was big for such a small creature, the horse bounded onto the bedside table, landing neatly beside Michael's untouched supper tray. After several hungry mouthfuls of stew, he was ready to reply.

"I am Sunkwaki, Spirit of the Horse Dance, son of Wakangli, warhorse of Chief Inkpaduta, pupil of the Keeper of Many Secrets, loyal servant of Wakan Tanka and – oops! – the guy who just spilled red wine on your tablecloth..." The horse hung his head apologetically. "But you can call me Hunter!"

As Hunter spoke, the great wizard's suspicious look changed to one of surprise. But there was more. "And I'm your transportation!"

As neatly as a champion steeplechaser, Hunter bounded down to the floor, where he began to grow bigger, taller and wider, more sleek and sinewy and more... real. Now, before Michael Scot, there stood a horse, made not of painted wood but of flesh and blood.

That night, like so many other nights, sleep did not protect Marnie from the visions she dreaded...

Michael Scot, dressed in his familiar, velvet robes spun round and round... In his eye sockets nestled ancient coins...

Marnie sat bolt upright in bed and cried out in fear.

"Are you OK?" called Kyle, from the far end of the attic. He flipped a light switch and tiptoed towards Marnie, who was clutching her head in her hands.

"Was it a bad dream?"

The Shoebox Zoo looked fearfully at each other, before clambering, slithering and fluttering onto their mistress's pillow.

"It was so weird," murmured Marnie from between her fingers. "It was Michael—"

"Michael?" interrupted Bruno. He scratched his furry head, a look of confusion in his warm, brown eyes. "I'd almost forgotten about Michael…"

"And he ssseemsss to have forgotten all about usss," Ailsa hissed.

Edwin flapped his wings crossly. "He's abandoned us to an uncertain fate far across the ocean—"

But Bruno disagreed. "Why would Michael abandon us?" he said. "He needs us to help Marnie find the Book!"

"I guess you're right," said Marnie quickly. She knew from experience that, left to their own devices, Edwin and the others were quite capable of bickering all night. And there were far more important things to discuss. "There's this dream I keep having," she explained. "It's at a wedding or something… and there are these tepees by a river."

Kyle looked intrigued. "A Native American wedding?" he asked. "What does this have to do with Michael and the Quest?"

"We need cluesss, Marnie!" said Ailsa urgently. "Proper cluesss!"

There was nothing Marnie would have liked

better than proper clues. She slumped back against her pillows disconsolately, looking at the anxious faces peering at her. It was all very well being the Chosen One, but she was finding the pressure increasingly hard to bear. Everyone expected her to be all seeing, all knowing and the greatest detective since Sherlock Holmes. But she wasn't. Once, she'd possessed the power to walk through a brick wall... now, she was just plain old Marnie McBride, who didn't have the power to find a single clue. But then...

Light began to emit from the torn page with a blinding intensity and the Native American pattern shimmered to reveal a line that wriggled, turned and looped until it became a picture of a snake. The light faded.

"What does it mean?" Marnie pondered. "First a horse rune, now a snake rune." Then it struck her. "But the snake is staying on the page. When I saw the horse rune, it faded."

"And I'm fading too," said Kyle, stifling a yawn. "Let's work this out in the morning."

Marnie nodded thoughtfully, then lay down to sleep. She didn't see the apparition appear outside the window or hear the menacing voice that whispered into the dark night.

"Goodnight, little ones."

It was Toledo.

Hunter thundered through the night, carrying Michael

47

Scot far into the forest to a clearing where a flickering campfire burned. Beside it sat the mysterious Native American.

As soon as the wizard slid to the ground, Hunter returned to being a wooden dance stick. Michael picked it up gently. "In over a hundred years, I have not been on such a fine horse," he said.

The other man nodded.

"Why do you invade my dreams, Nathaniel?" asked Michael as he slowly made his way over to the campfire. He handed over the dance stick.

Nathaniel regarded him solemnly for a moment, before chuckling. "Me, the invader?" he said. "We have dreams, visions too – we seek them. We call this the Vision Quest. It's kind of like the Quest of your Chosen One – our Chosen One too."

"The Quest is in danger, as we all are," said Michael urgently. "The evil of the Book grows each day."

"I know this," said Nathaniel calmly. "And what I also know is that there are a couple of kids who need your help. Maybe you messed up so badly before that you don't want to risk it again, but I'll tell you something. There comes a time when we've got to face up to our responsibilities."

When Michael Scot looked up, his dark eyes were full of remorse.

CHAPTER SIX

SNAKES ALIVE

Marnie groaned. How was she supposed to decide between a trip to the grocery store and 'fresh air and exercise'? As far as she was concerned, they both sucked.

"Well, you city kids aren't going to sit around here all day," announced Grandma. "Come on, there are lots of really neat trails around here." She handed a folded sheet of paper to Kyle, as if this proved her point.

Kyle politely spread out the trail map and his eyes lit up. "Snake Creek Trail!" he exclaimed.

"Where?" demanded Marnie. She checked out the map and grinned delightedly, thinking of the snake symbol that had appeared on the torn page. A proper clue at last!

Gramps wasn't so sure. "They don't call it Snake Creek Trail for nothing," he warned. "Don't go wandering off the path, OK?"

"We won't, Gramps!" said Marnie, hurriedly putting a sensible look on her face. But, inside, she was fizzing with excitement. The Quest continued!

An hour later, after tramping along a trail filled with buzzing flies, vicious mosquitoes and the sound of Kyle's incessant whingeing, it seemed as if the Quest had come to a grinding halt once more.

"Look, do you think it was *easy* for me to find those clues in Scotland?" said Marnie, swatting a stray branch out of her way. "No, it's a Quest. It's not supposed to be easy."

"I wasn't *with* you in Scotland, was I?" Kyle reminded her. "How should I know? And besides, we should be going *that* way." He pointed to the left.

"Whatever!" snapped Marnie. "If you'd read the map properly, you would know that *that* way is the *wrong* w—" She swung her head round as a curious rattling noise filled the air. "Ssh," she said cautiously. "Listen."

The noise sounded again, from the same direction as before. Mist had begun to weave in and out of the trees.

"What?" said Kyle grumpily. "I can't hear anything."

Marnie looked at him in disbelief. Did he think she was making this up? She angrily tossed her hair back and stomped off the trail, heading towards the strange noise.

"Where are you going?" called Kyle. "Remember what Gramps said about going off the path!"

Marnie ignored him. She had no time for scaredy cats, not when she was so close to discovering something really worthwhile.

"Fine!" Kyle shouted. "Do what you want!" He tramped back the way they'd come.

On the far side of Denver, an old man slowly dragged a golden mask from his greying head. He looked exhausted.

"You shouldn't, Master," McTaggart scolded softly. "You know it drains you."

Michael Scot ignored him. "I see the Chosen One has lost none of her stubborn qualities," he croaked.

Marnie marched on, deeper and deeper into the darkening wood, her feet crashing through the thick undergrowth. The rattling sound was getting louder and the mist was growing thicker. She must be close now. *Really* close.

"Marnie," the taunting call came from behind her.

She whipped round. There was no one there.

"Marnie!" This time it came from her left.

Suddenly, she knew with terrible certainty whose voice she could hear. But it couldn't be, could it? "Toledo?" she whispered, slowly turning round to face the impossible. There, between the shadowy trees, floated a ghostly, transparent Toledo. He was clad in a white, embroidered robe and his face wore its familiar supercilious expression.

"How good to see you again," said the Shapeshifter smoothly. "My, but you *do* look peaky… almost as if you've seen a ghost!" He laughed manically.

Marnie stared in horror. Her throat felt as if it was clutched in a vicelike grip and it was with difficulty she forced out words. "But you're dead… You *are* a ghost!"

"I only want to talk." Toledo's voice was saccharine-sweet. "I want to *help* you."

If there was one thing Marnie knew for certain, it was that the Shapeshifter didn't want to help her. He wanted the Book and the evil power that it contained. And only the Chosen One could open the Book. Marnie knew it. And he knew it.

Marnie backed away as the evil apparition glided towards her. "Get away from me!" she cried, turning to run. But she stumbled almost immediately, sprawling headlong across the forest floor, crisp with fallen leaves. Toledo loomed above her and she let out a piercing scream. Desperately, Marnie scrambled to her feet and staggered over the uneven ground. She had to get away from him!

But Toledo didn't follow. "Run along, little Chosen One," he mused. "I can wait. You'll see."

Marnie crashed through the undergrowth, with no idea where she was heading. Then her foot caught on a tree root and she tripped, tumbling over and over down a steep embankment. When she hit the bottom she collapsed in an unconscious heap, oblivious to the rattling sound that was growing louder. But the Shoebox Zoo, who had bounced from her backpack as it hit the ground, heard it. They also saw where the sound was coming from, and screamed in terror as a diamondback rattlesnake – its body as thick as a weightlifter's arm – crawled from beneath a nearby rock. It was heading straight for Marnie.

"We must save her or we are all doomed!" bellowed Bruno. He heaved a stone from the ground and hurled it at the deadly rattlesnake, thwacking it neatly between the eyes.

"Oh, well done, Bruno!" Edwin called, but a split-second later he was squawking incoherently as the angry snake slithered towards the Shoebox Zoo. It reared its massive head and was just about to strike when…

Whoosh!

Marnie was sure that she must be dreaming. Beneath her, she felt the smoothness of a soft quilt rather than the rough forest floor. And close by, she heard the gravely voice of Michael Scot. Cautiously, she opened her eyes to find that this was no dream.

"Oh, Master!" Edwin, Ailsa and Bruno shouted, bowing reverently.

"Be quiet!" came the sharp reply.

"Michael?" Marnie asked, thoroughly confused. The great wizard was so different from the last time she'd seen him. He looked older, shrunken even, and his skin seemed papery thin. Nevertheless, it *was* Michael.

"I—I thought you were in Scotland." She threw her arms around the wizard, who held her tight. "I just saw Toledo in the woods!" she gasped. "I thought he was dead!"

Michael and McTaggart exchanged an uneasy glance.

A horrible suspicion crept into Marnie's mind. "What's going on?" she asked, suddenly afraid of what she might hear.

"You *did* see him," explained Michael reluctantly. "He is shapeless, but he needs an empty vessel to fill, a body to inhabit. And if he does so, you must beware."

The delight at seeing Michael was rapidly being replaced by fear. Marnie couldn't help noticing that the Shoebox Zoo looked as frightened as she felt. "I don't understand," she whispered.

Michael took a deep shuddering breath. "There's something I should have told you..." he said, his voice wavering. "There's a second prophecy."

Marnie didn't have to be a mind reader to work out that a second prophecy was bad news. But she didn't have time to wonder why Michael had kept this secret, because McTaggart was reciting the dreadful words...

"But when the clock does chime again, and hours and minutes pass,

The cogs will turn relentlessly behind the cloudy glass,

Until the Dawn Queen's faithless hand shall open up the Book,

Then death and darkness will descend on all who dare to look…"

"The clock has struck again," murmured Michael. "Toledo is here, reborn and more powerful than ever."

"But who's the Dawn Queen?" asked Marnie. She thought she knew everything about the Book of Forbidden Knowledge, but this was totally new to her.

"She is like you – a Chosen One," said the wizard. "But she was chosen by evil… by the Book." He paused, his eyes wracked with pain and guilt. "Where she is or how she will rise again, I don't know."

"But now that you're here, everything will be OK, right?" asked Marnie hopefully. Then she remembered something that she had to tell him. "Michael, I had a dream about you – and you had pennies on your eyes."

McTaggart quickly looked away, but not before Marnie noticed that his eyes were wet with tears.

The great wizard was calm. "Sometimes," he murmured, "a dream is only a dream." He drew his hand over Marnie's eyes and…

…Marnie and the Shoebox Zoo were back in the forest. Totally disorientated, she looked around, surprised to see that they were at the bottom of the slope where she'd fallen.

Michael's disembodied voice echoed through the

trees. "Put your hand under the rock, child, and you will find what you seek."

Obediently, Marnie crouched down and reached her hand towards the large stone where the snake had lain in wait. She paused. This had to be one of the stupidest things she'd ever done. But Michael had said it was OK, so gingerly, she reached beneath the stone and her fingers closed around something long and feathery. With a huge sense of relief, she pulled out an ancient rattle. Gently, she shook it, to find that it sounded exactly like a rattlesnake...

"Weird..." she murmured. How was *this* going to help her find the Book?

Later that day, after a remorseful Kyle had come to find her and they'd trudged back home together through the forest, Marnie's grandma took her to one side.

"There's something I should have told you before," she began.

Marnie grinned expectantly. This was certainly a day of revelations.

"Your mom once had a set of animals just like your Shoebox Zoo," Grandma said. "We found them in this old junk shop in Denver on her eleventh birthday. She saw them in the window and she just fell in love with them. The old guy behind the counter wouldn't take a penny for them." She paused for breath, looking suddenly guilty. "But she was obsessed with them, you see... It was like they were changing her into

some other person. So I… I…"

"Go on," said Marnie gently. Somehow, she knew what was coming.

"I gave them back to the junk shop," admitted her grandma, her eyes full of sorrow.

"It's OK," said Marnie, flinging her arms around her grandma. She wasn't to know that Marnie's mother hadn't been able to wake the Shoebox Zoo, like Marnie. Nothing Grandma had or hadn't done would have changed the way things were. It was up to Marnie to unlock the secrets of *The Book of Forbidden Knowledge* and defeat the Dawn Queen, whoever she was.

CHAPTER SEVEN

The powwow

McTaggart pulled apart the heavy drapes that surrounded the four-poster bed. "So, sir, what'll it be for breakfast on this fine day?" he asked jovially. "Would you like a kipper with some freshly churned butter or would you prefer the full Scottish complement?"

The great wizard lay motionless. "You don't have to do this, McTaggart," he said quietly.

"Eleven hundred years I've served you," said his servant, his voice a mixture of pride and anguish. "I'm not about to stop now."

Michael's response was matter-of-fact. "You know I'm dying," he said. "You're free to do as you wish."

"The full complement it is then," replied McTaggart, closing the drapes before his face crumpled.

Deep in thought, his face wearing a look of utter

despair, McTaggart made his way down to the great kitchens of the Fairmont Springs Hotel, where he loaded a plate with sausages, bacon, eggs, black pudding and tomatoes. He placed this on a silver tray, to which he also added a pot of piping-hot tea and a tall glass of freshly squeezed orange juice. Then he began the long climb back to Room 1111.

But he had only reached the hotel lobby, when his master's voice rang out clear and loud. "McTaggart! Come quickly!"

The servant looked puzzled. "Where are you, Master?" he called anxiously.

"Over here!" The reply came from a high-backed armchair at the far end of the lobby. "Hurry! My power is fading!"

But when the servant reached the armchair, it was empty. Or was it? White smoke began to curl and swirl, slowly filling the chair to reveal a wraith-like figure, his eyes glowing with a terrible malevolence and his mouth set in a sneer.

"My dear McTaggart, after eleven hundred years, have you learnt nothing?" said the ghostly Toledo. "Are you so gullible that you have fallen for a cheap ventriloquist's trick?"

As if in slow motion, the breakfast tray slipped from McTaggart's numb fingers, crashing to the floor. Shocked into action, he turned to run. "Michael!" he shouted. "He's here!"

Toledo pointed lazily and a flash of electricity burst

forth from his elegant finger, streaming towards the fleeing servant. *Zap!* McTaggart was frozen in mid-air, a look of utter terror on his perfectly still face. He could do nothing to stop the Shapeshifter's smoky figure streaming across the lobby, up the stairs and out of sight.

Far away in Denver, Marnie, Gramps and Kyle had just arrived at the Powwow. Marnie could hardly wait for it to begin. Kyle had promised a festival to remember, with wild music, action-packed dancing and stalls. Kyle was taking part in one of the contests, performing a traditional Native American dance. But first, if she was to find out about the weird rattle, this was the place to do it.

They left Gramps beside the Native American art display and hurried across the field towards the brightly coloured tents.

"I mean, if I shook it and something happened…" Marnie sighed, giving the rattle an experimental shake, "we'd be getting somewhere, right?"

"Look, let's grab a drink and then we'll hook up with my cousin," said Kyle, heading for a refreshment stall. "He might be able to help."

Marnie nodded absent-mindedly as they joined the queue. "I guess it's just another one of Michael's little riddles," she continued. "A riddle within a riddle within a great big puzzle."

"Hey, Kyle!" interrupted a breathless voice.

All thoughts of the rattle, *The Book of Forbidden Knowledge* and even the Quest flew right out of Marnie's head as she realised who'd butted in. It was Becky, and her eyelashes fluttered madly at Kyle. Then her eyes met Marnie's.

"Oh." The disappointment in Becky's voice was unmistakable. "So you're here too."

"Yeah, sorry," said Marnie, not feeling at all apologetic.

"I'd better go and find Mom," Becky said hurriedly. "I just came over to say hi." She spun on her heel and hurried away.

"Hey, Becky!" shouted Kyle uselessly. He whipped round and glared at Marnie. "Can't you at least give her a chance?" he said.

Marnie couldn't believe her ears. Why was *she* suddenly the bad guy? "Excuse me!" she exploded. "I didn't exactly see her say, 'Hi, Marnie! Nice to see you!' But if you want to hang out with your girlfriend, that's fine with me. I've got better things to do." Angrily, she shoved a bottle of soda into Kyle's hand, snatched up her own drink and stormed away.

A low noise flowed around Room 1111. Michael Scot gathered his cloak about him. "McTaggart?" he said cautiously.

"Poor Michael Scot," Toledo's voice mocked him.

The great wizard started in horror. Glancing left and right, he grasped his magical staff, then quickly

61

dragged its tip around him, drawing a fiery circle on the stone floor.

"Signs and symbols, riddles and rhymes…" the disembodied voice echoed all around.

"Begone!" Michael shouted, turning his head this way and that, as the voice ebbed and flowed around him. "Remember who created you and the power he wields…"

Toledo's next words were chilling. "But your power is almost gone," he said.

Instantly, Michael Scot's glowing circle vanished and Toledo appeared from a cloud of white smoke.

"We're so similar, you and I," the Shapeshifter hissed. "Two sides of the same coin. The positive and the negative. As your power fades, so mine burns bright." Then, with a great whoosh, his ghostly shape rushed towards the great wizard, slamming into him.

Michael Scot fell.

Marnie McBride felt as if a great iron fist had punched her in the stomach. She buckled, helplessly flinging out her arms and sending her soda flying into the air. The bottle smashed to the ground, its pale liquid trickling away and her vision clouded.

Michael Scot turned round and round. He was dressed in his finest robes. In his eye sockets sat golden coins.

"Marnie!" Kyle's shout brought her whizzing back to the Powwow. Dazed, and totally clueless about what was happening, she followed him wordlessly towards a craft stall.

"Hey, Henry," said Kyle to the older boy in charge of the stall. "This is my *friend*, Marnie."

She realised that he was making a point, but Marnie didn't care now. Her weird experience had driven all thoughts of their argument from her mind.

"This is my cousin," said Kyle to Marnie. Henry grinned at her.

Marnie smiled back politely.

"Well…?" Kyle said. "The rattle?"

With difficulty, Marnie dragged her thoughts away from Michael Scot and back to the Powwow. "Oh, yeah," she said, reaching into her backpack. How could she have forgotten?

Henry turned the ancient rattle over and over in his hands. "Where did you get this?" he asked slowly.

"We found it under a rock on the Snake Creek Trail," Kyle said cagily. "What can you tell us about it?"

"Well, it probably belonged to a *wichasha wakan*," said Henry. "That's about all I can tell you, cuz." He handed it back, adding, "Oh, and it's worth *a lot* of money."

Marnie and Kyle thanked Henry and were walking away when a nearby loudspeaker crackled into life. "Young Men's Fancy Dance – start getting ready, please!" a cheerful voice announced.

"I'd better go and put my make-up on," said Kyle.

But Marnie caught his arm. There was something she needed to know. "What did he mean?" she asked.

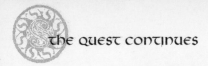

"He said it belonged to a *wich–wichasha…*"

"*Wichasha wakan*," said Kyle. "It's kind of hard to explain. It means *man of power* or *holy man*. It's what you'd call a *medicine man* – like your wizard, Michael Scot."

Michael Scot struggled to his feet, leaning heavily on his faithful staff. "You will never have the Book," he murmured shakily. "Only the hand of the Chosen One can touch it."

"Have you forgotten?" jeered Toledo. "There is another Chosen One – and her time draws near. Tick-tock, tick-tock…"

Outside, the wind suddenly gathered strength, blowing the hotel's windows wide and chilling the air. The great wizard sank to his knees.

"Ladies and gentlemen," boomed the loudspeaker inside the large tent. The audience rippled with excitement. "We begin with the grand entry, as we honour our flags, our peoples' past, our veterans, our elders and our leaders. Please rise as we pay tribute and homage to our beautiful culture."

Marnie rushed to her seat, stumbling over rough ground and collapsing onto Gramps.

"Woah, Marnie!" he said, catching her. "Are you OK?"

His granddaughter gulped. She'd never felt *less* OK, but she couldn't tell Gramps that. She nodded quickly and sank back against her seat, trying desperately to gather her tumultuous thoughts. If the rattle belonged to a type of wizard, did that mean it belonged to Michael Scot – or someone else…? What did this clue *mean*? And why had she felt such a physical blow earlier? Did this have something to do with the Quest too?

"Young Mens' Fancy!" interrupted the voice on the loudspeaker cheerily. "Ladies and gentlemen, this is the Young Mens' seven to twelve!"

At once, the rhythmic beating of drums filled the air and a crowd of brightly dressed boys burst into the tent, dancing wildly across the sawdust floor. One competitor stood out from the rest. The boy was clad in a magnificent Native American outfit decorated with fringes, feathers and a huge pair of eagle-like wings. On his head was a stunning headdress, while his face was painted with a single white stripe.

Marnie clapped as the dancer spun and whirled until he was a blur of colour. It wasn't until the boy slowed to look in her direction that she realised, to her astonishment, that it was Kyle. Now she clapped even louder. How come she'd never realised he was so good?

Marnie had the eerie feeling that she was being watched. She tore her eyes away from the display and scanned the crowd. She saw him at once. It was the old Native American from the airport, sitting directly across the aisle. He gave Marnie a mysterious smile. Shaken, she quickly looked back at the dancers.

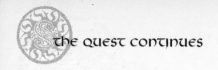

She wasn't the only one to recognise the old man. Three pairs of tiny eyes were watching him warily from the safety of Marnie's backpack.

"I've got a hunch *he* could tell usss about the rattle," hissed Ailsa, her eyes glowing with excitement. When the Native American rose from his seat and went through the tent's exit, she slid quickly after him. Bruno and Edwin had no choice but to follow.

But outside the display tent, the Shoebox Zoo quickly lost all hope of following the Native American, whose snakeskin boots had vanished into a forest of legs. Now, they were looking for a place to hide from the hundreds of enormous feet thudding all around, slithering, hopping and running for their lives.

Far away from the pounding drums and heaving crowds of the Powwow, Toledo was gaining the upper hand. He hovered menacingly over Michael Scot, who now lay motionless on the stone floor of Room 1111. Tiny white feathers fluttered down, landing on the wizard's deathly white face.

"Your time has come," whispered the Shape-shifter. He pointed an elegant finger and a stream of blinding light instantly coursed towards Michael Scot's forehead, draining the last of the great wizard's power.

And there was no one to stop him.

CHAPTER EIGHT

SECRETS REVEALED

Finally, Marnie was enjoying herself. The Powwow, with its dizzying kaleidoscope of colour and pounding rhythm had left no room for worries and riddles. She grabbed her backpack, eager to show Edwin, Ailsa and Bruno what was going on.

"You guys have got to see this!" she said, peering inside.

The backpack was empty.

"Well, what do we have here?" said Becky. She grinned slyly at the little stone bear standing proudly on the craft stall.

"Hi!" Kyle's cousin Henry popped up from behind the counter and Becky jumped. "Can I help you?" he asked.

"Er, yeah… I'm interested in this," said Becky, grabbing the bear. "And those two," she added, pointing to the metal eagle and patterned snake.

Henry looked as intrigued as Becky did about the three tiny creatures, which wasn't surprising – it was the first time he'd clapped eyes on the Shoebox Zoo. He gently took the bear from Becky and turned it over in his hands, sucking his breath through his teeth as he examined it. "Yeah, well, these guys are real special," he said casually to Becky.

"There you are!" shrieked Aurora Dexter as she rushed towards Becky, stumbling in her too-high heels. "I've been looking everywhere for you!" Starbeam TV's resident psychic skidded to a halt next to the stall.

"Perfect timing, Mom!" said Becky, casting a scheming glance at her mother. "Just take a look at these – aren't they beautiful?"

Aurora's eyes locked onto the eagle and she became suddenly still. "Strange, magical," she murmured. "How… how much are they?"

"Like you said, lady," Henry said quickly, "they're strange and magical. I can't let you have them for less than five hundred dollars."

"I'll give you two fifty," barked Aurora as she plucked a purse from her handbag and began counting out notes.

Henry grinned widely. "You've got yourself a deal!" he said, curling a sheet of bubble-wrap around the eagle.

As Marnie looked towards the craft stall, her disbelief turned to anger. "Hey!" she cried, watching in astonishment as Henry popped a lumpy package into a carrier bag and began to wrap Bruno. "What are you *doing*?"

"Hi," said Aurora, totally ignoring the incensed look on Marnie's face. "What a coincidence bumping into you here." She paused and tilted her head to one side. "But then again, there's no such thing as coincidence. Everything is *meant* to happen."

Marnie grabbed Ailsa from the counter. "Well, this was *not* meant to happen!" she snapped. "Those guys are *mine*."

Aurora was calm, but firm. "I'm sorry," she said. "This gentleman is selling them to me."

A wave of fury flooded through Marnie and she snatched the carrier bag from Henry, hurriedly wedging Ailsa between Edwin and Bruno. "You can't sell something that isn't for sale!" she said, pushing the carrier into her backpack. "They're mine!" And she ran.

Marnie dodged between tents and stalls, but no matter where she went, the angry shouts followed close behind. What she needed was somewhere to hide. But where?

"In here," said a man's voice – it came from a large, colourful tepee. Without hesitation, Marnie pulled open the heavy canvas flap and slipped inside.

Her pursuers arrived just seconds later and plunged after her, staring in disbelief. The tent was packed with

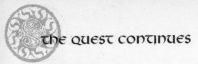

Native American men, changing into their outfits.

There was no sign of Marnie McBride.

To her amazement, Marnie found that instead of standing inside a tepee, she was outside – in the middle of a wood. A pale daylight flashed between the branches above, while a silvery mist weaved its way around the trunks. Crackling, snapping, spitting noises came from a blazing campfire in a small, bright clearing. And there, beside the leaping flames, the old Native American sat, perched on a fallen log.

"I thought you'd never get here, daughter," he said, his lined face friendly and welcoming. "Come by the fire and warm up."

Marnie hung back suspiciously, not sure what to think.

"You're in the world of spirits," explained the old man. "But don't worry, you're safe here. No harm will come to you, not as long as I'm around."

There was a time that Marnie would have been seriously freaked out by these words, but that was long ago, before the Quest. Now, she took a deep breath and obediently went to sit beside the fire. A carved wooden horse caught her eye and absent-mindedly she picked it up, turning it over in her hands. "But who are you?" she asked the man.

There was a rustling and popping noise. "Thank goodness for that!" gasped Bruno, fighting his way clear of bubble-wrap and poking his head out of

Marnie's backpack. "I was suffocating in there. Oh, it's *you!*" Dumbfounded, he stared at the Native American.

"What?" spluttered Marnie in disbelief. "You guys *know* each other?" She glared at Bruno as Edwin and Ailsa crept sheepishly out of the backpack to join him.

"He said he was going to turn us into monster meat if we told anyone!" protested Edwin.

"He's telling you the truth," said the Native American calmly. "I needed to be sure that you were the One. The girl child spoken of by the ancestors." He dealt the final blow. "The Chosen One who seeks the Book."

The Shoebox Zoo gasped.

To Marnie, it suddenly seemed as if everything had gone still. She'd thought that this man was against her. Now it appeared that he'd been on her side all along. "The Chosen One?" she whispered. "And you know about the Book too?"

"That Book is like a shadow on my heart, bearing down on the hoop of my people," the old man continued. "I can guide you, daughter, but the path is yours and yours alone." He looked up solemnly. "The help you once relied on is no more."

Marnie stared at the Native American with growing unease. She thought back to the strange blow she'd felt earlier and reproached herself for not realising sooner that it was connected with the great wizard. Something was very wrong – she knew it. "What's happened to Michael?" she demanded.

The old man's next words explained nothing – and everything. "Things change, child. Nothing remains the same."

Back at the Powwow, Marnie found herself in big trouble.

"You didn't even stay till the end of my dance!" stormed Kyle, who was back in his everyday clothes now. "I thought you'd be excited to come to the Powwow and watch me dance, but you just wanted to find out about your stupid rattle!"

Marnie hung her head. "Look, Kyle," she began. "it's a long story, OK?"

"Oh, yeah?" said Kyle sarcastically.

But as she was about to explain, Gramps appeared, quickly gathering her into a hug. "Where were you?" he asked. Then, without waiting for a reply, "Kyle came first place in the Fancy Dance!"

Feeling really guilty that she'd missed so much, Marnie glanced over at Kyle. He gave a small grin, his cheeks flushed with embarrassment.

"You'd have been so proud of him," Gramps said. "It was *fantastic.*"

A flash of energy zapped through the lobby of the Fairmont Springs Hotel, bringing McTaggart back to life and releasing him from imprisonment at last. He resumed his race for the stairs, pounding up, up, up towards Room 1111. "Michael!" he shouted. "I'm coming."

But when McTaggart flung back the heavy wooden door, he caught his breath. The great wizard lay motionless on the floor, his hands folded across his chest as if in death.

"Master!" cried the faithful servant, dropping to his knees and touching the wizard's cold forehead. "Wake up, master!"

Michael Scot's eyes fluttered open and the servant heaved a sigh of relief, but his joy was short-lived. "My time has come, old friend," Michael murmured sadly. "My science and knowledge have failed the Chosen One."

"You haven't failed her!" protested McTaggart. "We've got work to do!" He looked around frantically. "The staff, where's your staff?"

"It's too late," said his master. "His powers are beyond me now. You must help Marnie. She needs you. He paused, as if each word cost him dearly. "Trust Nathaniel. His is the only power that can help her."

McTaggart dug his fingers into the great wizard's velvet cloak. "Don't leave me!" he pleaded. "You can't leave me to do this on my own…"

"You must not fail the Chosen One," whispered Michael. "If the Dawn Queen opens the Book, there will be nothing. Only darkness…" As his voice faded, so did Michael Scot. His papery skin grew translucent, slowly disappearing from sight until all that remained of the greatest wizard who ever lived was a battered old cloak.

McTaggart threw his arms wide and let out a great cry of anguish. "*Michael*," he wailed. "*Michael*."

By the time they arrived home it was dark, and Marnie was tired and edgy. As she walked into the kitchen, the lights flickered.

Michael Scot turned slowly around and around, a gold coin tucked into each of his eye sockets.

She opened her eyes and, for the second time that day, felt shockwaves run through her, as if something had rammed into her stomach. The dish she was holding slipped to the ground, shattering into countless pieces.

Grandma appeared in the doorway. "Are you OK?" she said anxiously, putting an arm round Marnie's shoulders.

"I'm fine," lied Marnie, her ragged breathing slowly returning to normal.

Bang! The toaster exploded, sending a shower of sparks cascading into the air and jangling Marnie's nerves yet again.

"That generator has a life of its own," said Grandma, shaking her head with exasperation.

Marnie glanced at the tattered shed, rumbling ominously across the yard. She didn't reply.

hunter to
the rescue

aylight was beginning to filter between the trees
when the old Native American appeared. He
crept slowly across the clearing and crouched beside
one corner of the blackened shed, reaching for the
charred bunch of herbs that lay there. Swiftly repeat-
ing an ancient ritual, he pulled a fresh bunch of sage
from his pocket, sparked a match and touched it to the
herbs. He left the fragrant bunch smouldering beside
the shed.

At the Fairmont Springs Hotel, McTaggart was beginning to grieve. He hadn't moved from the spot where
his master had died and now stared blankly at the cloak
and staff Michael Scot had left behind. White feathers
lay in small forlorn heaps on the stone floor.

"Dear me," taunted the Shapeshifter's voice. "Still
moping, McTaggart? What did the miserable old devil

ever do for you, hmm? Did he ever give you his trust? His friendship? After eleven hundred years of service, did he even give you his thanks?"

The servant snapped out of his trance and stared balefully around the darkened room. "What do you want from me?" he growled through gritted teeth.

Toledo spoke sweetly. "What should any master want from his servant?"

An outraged McTaggart stumbled to his feet. "I'm not your slave!" he shouted into the empty air. "I'll *never* be your slave! Michael gave me my freedom!"

"Oh, you *are* a slave – at least until the Book is found," replied Toledo. "Until then, you shall serve *me*!"

"I'd rather have another eleven hundred years of imprisonment than serve you!" McTaggart spat out the words bitterly.

With an angry roar, the Shapeshifter materialised, his wraithlike body looming overhead. "Then you shall *watch*!" he thundered, pointing at the cowering servant. A bolt of energy fizzed from his outstretched finger and – *flash!* – McTaggart was transformed into a white weasel, trapped inside an ornate gold cage. The little creature ran to and fro, frantically looking for a way out. "You shall watch," continued Toledo, his voice growing louder and more terrible, "with the pink, helpless eyes of a snivelling weasel while Juan Roberto Montoya de Toledo fulfils his destiny, claims the Book… and becomes the *Dawn Queen!*" His harsh laughed echoed around Room 1111.

Marnie turned feverishly in her sleep, throwing out one arm and knocking the torn page from her bedside table. As soon as it hit the floor, the page came alive, glowing with colour.

It was Edwin who spotted it. "Wake up!" he squawked, gesticulating wildly with his good wing. "It's another clue! It's writing a new rune!"

Waking with a start, Marnie peered over the edge of the bed and squinted blearily at the page. A strange symbol burned brightly – five jagged marks pointing from a palm-shaped centre.

Kyle had the answer. "It's a bear claw," he said, rubbing his eyes sleepily.

"Maybe it means that we've got to find a bear?" suggested Bruno.

"I wouldn't recommend going looking for one," said Kyle quickly.

Marnie couldn't agree more. She sprang out of bed, grabbing her backpack from a corner of the loft room. "And that's exactly why you guys had better behave yourselves," she said, briskly unzipping her bag and popping Bruno, Edwin and Ailsa inside. The last thing she needed was for the Shoebox Zoo to be charging off on their own and confronting wild bears. The Quest was dangerous enough already.

"Come on," she said to Kyle. "We've got a new clue to investigate!"

After cereal, orange juice and a heap of syrupy pancakes, they were ready to go. Marnie proudly wheeled an old-fashioned bicycle across the clearing and propped it beside Kyle's shiny new mountain bike.

Marnie's grandparents strolled over to take a look. "There's still life in that old bike," Gramps said fondly. "Your mom used to ride it all over the place—" He stopped mid-sentence and glanced across at Grandma, who was frowning at him.

"It's OK," Marnie said softly. "I know it used to be Mom's bike and it makes me feel good, not sad."

Grandma forced a smile and thrust a bulging lunch bag into Marnie's hand. "Well, make sure you guys get back before sundown," she said. "We don't want to have to send out any search parties!"

"Sure, Mrs Campbell!" said Kyle, fastening the clasp on his cycle helmet.

"Thanks, Grandma." Marnie pushed the lunchbag into her backpack, which was safely strapped to the back of the bike. She wasn't taking any chances – there was no way she was going to lose her backpack again. "See you!" she called, as she and Kyle pedalled away.

Marnie couldn't remember the last time she'd enjoyed herself so much. She raced after Kyle along the winding trail, dodging low branches and leafy obstacles in her way. The ground was rocky and uneven, which made the ride even more thrilling.

But the Shoebox creatures were having a dreadful time. They gazed in horror out of the backpack, at the woodland scene flashing past. In her hurry to be off, Marnie had forgotten to close the zip… Now, with every dip and every bump, the creatures were being thrown closer and closer to the gaping hole.

"Sssssssslow dowwwwwn!" hissed Ailsa.

But Marnie didn't hear. The wind rushing past her ears totally drowned out the snake's tiny voice.

"Come on, slow poke!" shouted Kyle.

Marnie pedalled faster still, her ancient bike bouncing over a large rock and thumping heavily to the ground. Undaunted, she zoomed away, totally unaware that she'd left three little creatures sprawling on the ground behind her.

Ailsa recovered first. "Wait!" she cried, as Marnie and Kyle rocketed away, disappearing into the distance.

"Arrrghhh! We're lost!" Edwin squawked hysterically. "Lost! Abandoned! We'll be eaten alive by wild beasts! *Help!*"

Bruno's eyes goggled as he looked at the wildly hopping eagle. "Your wing, Edwin," he said. "Where's your *wing*?" It was true. Edwin's clunky metal wing had vanished.

Edwin turned his head and let out a piercing shriek. "My wing!" he screeched. "I've lost my wing! *Arrrghhh!*"

"If you don't ssstop it," warned Ailsa, "we *will* be eaten by wild beassstsss!"

"Sssssh!" said Bruno, clamping a paw over Edwin's beak.

Suddenly, there was an ominous rustling noise, accompanied by the sound of cracking twigs. A deep growl reverberated through the woods and then the ground shook as an enormous grizzly bear burst from the undergrowth. It reared up on its hind legs, towering high above the terrified Shoebox Zoo, opened its great jaws and let out an ear-splitting roar.

Marnie's brakes squealed in protest as her bike skidded to a halt. Kyle pulled up beside her and gasping for breath they gazed around at the beautiful, sun-dappled glade. But the idyllic moment didn't last.

"Your backpack!" exclaimed Kyle.

Twisting round in her saddle, Marnie stared at the open backpack. Cursing her stupidity, she wrenched the bag free and peered inside. Gone. They were all gone! "We've got to find them!" she said.

Kyle nodded anxiously.

As they spun their bikes around, tiny hoofbeats clip-clopped into the clearing. Stunned, they looked down at the tiny horse.

"You'd better get a move on, or else you'll miss all the fun," he said cheerily. Then, shaking his mane impatiently, he galloped in the direction that they'd come. Marnie and Kyle followed in silence, pedalling furiously after the little horse.

Then they saw it. A huge grizzly bear – taller than a man, probably taller than *two* men – stood on its hind legs. Its roar was truly deafening. Edwin, Ailsa and Bruno cowered at its feet.

The miniature horse galloped fearlessly towards the great beast, rearing, stamping and neighing for all it was worth. But it was the sight of Marnie and Kyle that seemed to startle the grizzly. It turned and loped off.

"Go and pick on somebody your own size!" the horse shouted at the bear's large furry behind.

"And who might you be?" asked Edwin primly. He spotted his missing wing and plugged it back into its socket, before shaking his metal plumage importantly at the new arrival.

The little horse proudly introduced himself. "I am Sunkwaki, Spirit of the Horse Dance, son of Wakangli, warhorse of Chief Inkpaduta, pupil of the Keeper of Many Secrets, loyal servant of Wakan Tanka and the guy who just got you out of one heap of trouble!" He gave a toothy grin. "But you can call me Hunter."

Marnie grinned at the tiny rescuer. "Hey, Hunter," she said. "How did you know that we were in trouble?"

"I didn't," said Hunter, flinging back his bristly mane. "*He* did."

And there, slowly walking towards them, was the old Native American man.

"Grandpa?" said Kyle, his mouth wide with surprise.

Marnie spun round and stared at her best friend. "He's your *grandpa*...?" she croaked, her voice almost deserting her.

Kyle whipped his head round and stared back at Marnie. "You *know* him?" he asked incredulously

"We kind of met at the Powwow," explained the old man. "But we've never been formally introduced."

"Nathaniel Stone Horse… Marnie McBride," murmured Kyle.

"It's a pleasure to meet you properly," said Nathaniel, a smile transforming his face into a mass of crinkles.

"Likewise," said Marnie, smiling back. Now she knew beyond doubt that the old Native American was on her side. He was Kyle's grandfather.

Then Nathaniel's face became serious. "Just because you're looking for a bear clue," he said sternly to Marnie and Kyle, "doesn't mean you need to find yourselves a real bear. And you guys should know better than to fool around in these woods, with bears and who knows what else on the loose."

It was true. Marnie felt suddenly sheepish and she avoided Nathaniel's knowing gaze.

Kyle hung his head. "Sorry, Grandpa," he murmured.

"You might find that the quickest way home is straight across The Flats," said Nathaniel, as he turned to leave. The old Native American walked swiftly between the trees, leaves crunching beneath his snake-skin boots.

Then he was gone.

CHAPTER TEN

CRANSFORMACION

Toledo floated around Room 1111, his ghostly form as insubstantial as an early-morning mist. Slowly and deliberately, he scanned Room 1111, taking in the heavy wooden furniture and blood-red drapes. "It's so dismal in here," he groaned, curling his lip in disgust. "The great wizard didn't exactly have a flair for interior design, did he? No, that must have been a talent invested in me."

The Shapeshifter closed his eyes and regally swept a hand across the hotel room. As he did so, all that was dark and brooding became brilliant white – walls, curtains, floor, furniture. Everything except the weasel's gilt cage, which changed into glittering glass.

McTaggart the weasel became agitated, scampering around its transparent prison. "There must be a way out!" he squeaked.

Toledo ignored the frantic weasel and casually

snapped his fingers. Instantly, the plasma screen on the wall came alive.

"Until the next time," Starbeam TV's resident psychic was saying, "when Aurora Dexter takes you... *Above and Beyond!*"

"Above, beyond and together, my dear, we will fulfil the second prophecy," said Toledo loudly. And his monstrous laugh echoed around the gleaming room.

As soon as the bell rang to signal the end of filming, Aurora slumped in her chair, her face etched with frustration and despair.

"That's a wrap!" announced the studio manager. Then he chuckled. "Where do you *get* this stuff from?"

"Would you just—?" Aurora snarled angrily, but she was interrupted by a melodic ringing tone. Quickly, she hurried across the studio and flipped open her mobile phone. "Yes?" she barked.

The voice on the other end of the line was as smooth as silk and as American as the Wild West. "Hi. It's Robert Johns, Vice-president of Production, Channel 411," he said. "But you can call me Johnny. I was just passing through and I happened to catch your show."

"You saw my show?" breathed Aurora.

"Now, you have a terrific little show and I just cannot leave town without meeting you," he continued. "Are you free this evening?"

"This evening?" said Aurora. She looked up and mouthed a silent 'thank you' towards the ceiling.

"I'm leaving town tomorrow," said Johnny briskly. "Destiny doesn't deliver a chance like this twice."

Aurora's smile was a mixture of triumph and elation. "If it's Destiny, then why should I stand in its way?" she said.

"So, dinner at my place. I'll send a car." The man's voice was firm. "It'll be so wonderful to meet you."

As Aurora hung up, Toledo gave an oily smile of triumph.

Marnie and Kyle rode steadily through the wood, the afternoon sun slanting through the trees now.

"So is he...?" began Marnie hesitantly. "I mean... He's at the airport. He's in the middle of the woods when I... when I walk into a tepee at the Powwow..." She paused and then stared right at Kyle. "Is he, you know—?"

"Is he one of those wishy-washy things?" interrupted Edwin's voice impatiently from the depths of Marnie's backpack.

Kyle looked annoyed. "A *wichasha wakan*?" he said. "A medicine man? Yeah, sure, let's just tell everyone, why don't we?"

"But how come you *couldn't* tell me?" asked Marnie. She felt puzzled by Kyle's attitude and more than a little hurt. He wasn't embarrassed about his grandfather, was he?

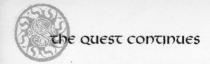

"I don't want to talk about it," said Kyle, then quickly corrected himself. "I mean, we're not *supposed* to talk about this stuff."

An eerie noise silenced them. It sounded like a church bell, gently tolling in the wind. But as far as Marnie knew, there was no church in these woods. She glanced at Kyle and as their eyes met, Marnie saw that he was as surprised as she was. In unspoken agreement, they moved cautiously forward.

Among the gently swaying trees was an old, wooden cross and, behind, the rotted remains of an old, wooden church. Low sunlight bathed the scene with a warm glow and Marnie felt an odd sense of calm. They tiptoed between the broken pews. And then they saw it. On the crumbling altar, there lay a book.

"Is it *the* Book?" breathed Kyle.

Marnie was doubtful. "I think *The Book of Forbidden Knowledge* is going to be a little more difficult to find," she replied. But still, it took all her courage to approach the altar and run her fingers over the ornate leather cover. Nothing happened, and she breathed a sigh of relief.

"What kind of book *is* it?" Kyle asked.

Carefully lifting the heavy cover, Marnie revealed page after page of old-fashioned writing. "It's a parish register," she said. "Births, marriages and—"

"Deaths!" chorused the Shoebox Zoo, who had somehow wriggled their way out of the backpack.

They clambered up onto the altar.

A light breeze fluttered the curled, yellow pages and Marnie shivered…

A hand touched the Book… The pioneer and the Native American girl stood before the old chief as he blessed their marriage… All three joined hands…

Marnie's eyes refocused and she placed her index finger on the register, running it slowly across the page. "Look!" she exclaimed, reading the words before her. "It says that on the eleventh day of the eleventh month, 1811, a marriage took place between Angus Alexander McBride and the daughter of Chief Stone Bear of the Lakota people. And look – there's the chief's mark!"

Edwin, Ailsa, Bruno and Kyle looked to where Marnie was pointing. It was roughly drawn, but unmistakable – a bear claw.

"Maybe these are the people in your dream," said Kyle quietly.

Marnie nodded. The pioneer of her visions looked so like her father because he was her father's *ancestor*. And the Native American had the same name as Kyle's grandfather. The two Stone Bears must be related too. The truth was almost too incredible to believe. Kyle was no longer just her best friend. He was her cousin too. Their lives were linked by *The Book of Forbidden Knowledge*.

Aurora Dexter stepped out of the gleaming white

limousine and gazed up at the floodlit towers of the Fairmont Springs Hotel. She smoothed bejewelled fingers over her long, flowing dress, glittering with sequins.

"Thank you," she said, turning to speak to the chauffeur. "Can you wait for a—"

But the hotel forecourt was deserted. Somehow, the car and its driver had vanished. Aurora drew a deep, shuddering breath. "OK, pull yourself together," she muttered. "Do you want your own show or not?" She drew herself up to her full height and, with her head held high, marched towards the magnificent entrance. But, once inside, Aurora's courage seemed to desert her once more. She ventured inside the empty lobby timidly – a small, frightened figure surrounded by shadows.

"Come on up!" The voice that Aurora recognised as belonging to the Vice-president of Production from Channel 411 echoed down the stairwell. "Room 1111."

Warily, Aurora obeyed. When she reached the door to Room 1111, she discovered that it was ajar. The psychic slipped inside the snow-white room. "Hello?" she called.

"Take a seat, my dear." The charming voice was polite, but firm.

After looking without success for the elusive TV executive, Aurora sat on a high-backed chair by the long dining table. In front of her was a sheet of thick, white paper covered in tiny writing.

"Eyes closed," said Toledo, his ghostly, terrible shape forming behind the chair.

Aurora jumped. "But I can't read what it says with my eyes shut, Johnny," she protested.

"A contract is a contract," replied the Shapeshifter, an undercurrent of menace now evident in his voice. "Don't you trust your new boss at Channel 411?"

Obediently, Aurora shut her eyes. "Sure I trust you," she said nervously.

"We sponsor your new show, you talk to the dear departed, become an A-list celebrity and we all make lots of money." Toledo paused dramatically as a wide grin split his villainous face. "That's after your fair hand has opened up *The Book of Forbidden Knowledge*, of course."

"What Book?" asked Aurora.

"Just part of your new show," Toledo murmured in her ear. "Now, you want this show more than anything, don't you?"

Aurora nodded frantically. "I want it more than anything!" she said.

"You want this show to reach into every corner of every home from coast to coast, don't you?" The voice grew louder and more insistent with every word.

"Across the length and breadth of the country... of the *world*!" cried Aurora, bright spots of colour appearing on each cheek as she grew increasingly excited.

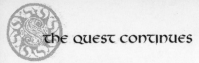

"I want it all!"

"Then sign," said Toledo.

The nib of the fountain pen scratched loudly in the silence as Aurora scrawled her name.

Toledo drew closer and peered over Aurora's shoulder and read the messy signature. His voice was loud and triumphant. "Together we will find the Book and fulfil our destiny and become *the Dawn Queen!*" He looked approvingly at Aurora. "My body, my new life…" he crooned.

Aurora stiffened. "You're scaring me," she said, fear creeping into her voice. "I don't know what you mean!" Her eyes snapped open and she whirled round, screaming with terror as she saw the spectre that hovered in the air.

On the far wall of Room 1111, the hands of a white, marble clock began to spin furiously, whizzing past strange hieroglyphics and coming to rest on the number eleven. Only then did Toledo speak, his voice filled with foreboding.

"But when the clock does chime again, and hours and minutes pass,

The cogs will turn relentlessly behind the cloudy glass,

Until the Dawn Queen's faithless hand shall open up the Book,

Then death and darkness will descend on all who dare to look…"

Toledo's cold eyes locked onto Aurora. "*From my watery grave you have summoned me,*" he hissed, "*and together we will fulfil our destiny!*"

The Shapeshifter transformed into a white mist and lurched towards his victim, his eyes alight with pure evil, snaking around her, whirling faster and faster, before disappearing into her shaking body.

There was a blinding flash.

When the air cleared, Aurora Dexter was still standing in exactly the same spot but everything about her had changed. Her expression was no longer desperate, but calm and focussed. Her colourful dress had been replaced with a sophisticated white suit. Her hair, once a tumble of curls, was swept up into a sleek chignon. She was utterly transformed.

"You're no longer trailer trash, Aurora Dexter," she said lazily, with more than a hint of Toledo in her voice. "From now on, it's prime-time TV, with your own show on Channel 411 – nationwide!"

Moonlight shone down on the clearing, revealing the old, wooden shed. It's doors stood wide open. Marnie McBride peered apprehensively at the throbbing, heaving monster that lay within.

"Don't go in there…" whispered a familiar voice. It was soft but urgent.

Marnie turned round, but there was no one there. As she looked back at the generator, the slimy golden tentacles of an octopus poked out from behind the machine, reaching towards her. She felt an irresistible urge to move forward, but the voice

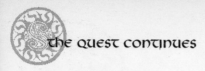

interrupted again.

"Not now." And Marnie suddenly realised that the voice belonged to Wolfgang! His familiar face appeared, wreathed in smoke and fire. "It's too soon," he said. "You *mustn't* go in there."

The little wolf melted away and in his place appeared Michael Scot, pennies balanced in his eye sockets…

Marnie arched out of bed to find that she was sweating, panting and shaking with fear.

She hoped desperately that she'd been dreaming.

CHAPTER ELEVEN

The Terrible Truth

Marnie stared listlessly at her half-finished breakfast, lost in thought. They were really starting to get to her now – dreams, visions, *whatever* they were. More importantly, what did they mean?

"Are you going to eat that, pumpkin?" asked Gramps, his fork hovering.

With a start, Marnie snapped out of her reverie. "Oh, sure. Help yourself," she murmured, watching her grandfather spear a sausage. "I had this dream," she said slowly. "It was about a man with pennies in his eyes… Is that a sign or a symbol or something?"

Gramps looked at her warily and paused before replying. "Well, when somebody has pennies in their eyes, it means that they've… well… it means that they've passed over."

Marnie stared straight ahead. She could feel the tears filling her eyes, but was unable to do anything about it.

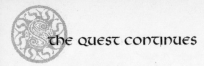

"Marnie?" said Grandma urgently. "Marnie!"

Michael Scot was dead.

Marnie blindly stumbled to her feet. "I don't feel very well," she mumbled, heading for her room. As she climbed the stairs, she heard her grandma's raised voice.

"See! This is what happens when you take the poor kid to a show where they talk to dead people."

The Shoebox Zoo watched sadly as tear after tear rolled down Marnie's cheeks, while the Chosen One was struggling to comprehend the awful truth: she was alone. And Toledo was back.

"Maybe it *was* just a dream," said Bruno hopefully.

"Pennies on the eyes are used to pay Kharon the ferryman to row the departed soul across the River Styx to Hades!" he wailed. "Don't you remember? We studied it in our Greek class with Michael *himself.*"

"It's all so long ago," sighed Bruno, hanging his head.

There was a gentle knock at the door. "Are you feeling any better?" called Grandma. "You don't want to miss Kyle's party, do you?"

A birthday party was the last thing she needed. But Marnie knew that, whatever had happened, Kyle was her best friend and she couldn't miss it. "Yeah, I'm feeling a lot better," she called, in what she hoped was a convincing voice. "I'm going to get ready now!"

"Wow!" Becky stared in amazement as she followed her mother through the luxurious lobby of the Fairmont Springs Hotel. "Are we really going to be living here?"

"That's right, honey," said Aurora, her voice brisk and businesslike. "Suite 1111."

"It's weird how there are no staff," said Becky, pulling her denim jacket tighter. "And why are you talking so weird?" she added suspiciously.

"Weird?" Aurora held up manicured hands in mock surprise. "I don't know what you mean."

"All fancy and stuff," said Becky. "And that cheesy business suit, Mom. It really *isn't* you."

Aurora spun round on her white stilettos to face Becky. When she spoke, her words were slow and deliberate. "Your mom is going to be the face of *Above and Beyond the Beyond*, networked across the nation," she said. "I can't very well appear in front of 24 million people looking like something the cat dragged in from Palookaville, can I?" She swept up the stairs, her heels clicking loudly. "Now, stop being such a moody teenager and come on!"

"But I'm not a teenager," whined Becky, tramping after her. "I'm only eleven."

Once upstairs, Aurora wrenched open the doors to the dazzling suite. "There, isn't this just wonderful!" she exclaimed.

"But it's all… white," said Becky, screwing up her face. "*Everything's* white."

95

Aurora nodded proudly. "Nice Mr Robert Johns has even laid on a complimentary pet for you – a cute little white weasel!" She walked swiftly to the far corner of the room and stiffened as she saw the empty glass container. "*Caramba! Se ha escapado!*" she roared. "Can't you see? McTaggart has flown the coop!"

Becky's eyebrows scrunched together. "The weasel's called McTaggart?" she murmured in disbelief. "And you can speak Spanish?"

But her mother was too busy to hear, dragging back curtains and scattering cushions in her wake, as she systematically searched the gleaming white room. Becky shrugged and began pulling party clothes – not white, but candyfloss pink – from her suitcase.

"Relax!" said Becky, fumbling with buttons. "I never wanted a weasel anyway. Rodents are not exactly my scene." She dragged up the zip of her cardigan, plucked a glittering tube from her bag and carefully applied a perfect pout of rosy lipgloss. "Can we go now?" she asked.

"Go where?" said Aurora. She looked at Becky's outfit with disapproval. "Can't you wear something a little more… *white*?"

"It's Kyle's birthday party!" said Becky impatiently. "I told you last week, Mom. You promised to take me."

"Kyle?" said Aurora distractedly, as she peered inside a tiny drawer. "Who's Kyle?"

Becky blushed as pink as her clothes. "That really cute boy in my class," she said. "The one who came to the studio?"

"Who else will be there?" Aurora's attention was fixed firmly on her daughter now.

"I don't know," said Becky, shrugging her shoulders. "A whole bunch of people – Kyle's friends from school, that girl who went to Scotland—"

As if the sun had suddenly appeared from behind storm clouds, Aurora's face brightened. "Marnie's going to be there?" she asked, already heading towards the door. "What are we waiting for?"

Becky rolled her eyes and trudged after her mother.

Marnie sat in front of the mirror, feeling totally drained. She could sense that the Shoebox Zoo were waiting for her to come up with a grand plan, but dabbing on make-up was all she could manage without bursting into tears again.

"What'll become of usss now?" whispered Ailsa. "We'll never be human again."

"We're done for," said Bruno.

"*Doomed*!" cried Edwin, flinging his wings in the air.

It was anger that brought Marnie back to life. She whirled to face the tiny creatures. "Michael is dead – and all you can think about is *yourselves*?" she said slowly.

Ailsa was unrepentant. "It'sss all very well for you, Marnie. You're human already. But what'll happen to usss now?"

"We're going to stay exactly as we are – poor students locked in these ridiculous bodies – and all you can think about is a stupid party!" added Edwin.

Marnie hadn't thought of it quite like this. "It's Kyle's twelfth birthday," she said. "I can't miss it."

"We're not exxxactly in the party mood," said Ailsa.

Marnie let out a long sigh. "It's like when my mom died," she said, more softly now. "There's a choice we can make. We can cry and sit around feeling sad and sorry for ourselves, or we can carry on."

"But we don't even know how Michael died, or where, or when…" said Bruno.

A sob rose in Marnie's throat but with a great effort, she quelled it. "I know," she replied. "But we're not going to find out by sitting around here, are we?"

There was a sound at the bedroom door, not a knocking, but a weird scrabbling, scratching noise.

"Is it Hunter?" said Ailsa, twirling her tail with excitement.

Bruno shook his head. "That's a real creature. And it's got sharp claws."

"What does it want?" squawked Edwin.

There was only one way to find out. Marnie went for it, striding over to the painted wooden door and wrenching it open. At once, a white weasel darted across the carpet.

"It'sss a rat!" shrieked Ailsa. "A rat! A rat! A rat!" Petrified, she and the rest of the Shoebox Zoo scattered.

"It's OK, you guys," said Marnie, calmly picking it up. "It's a weasel, not a rat. And it's cute."

"It's me!" squeaked a tiny voice that sounded curiously like—

"McTaggart?" said Marnie incredulously. The last time she'd seen Michael Scot's servant, he'd been much taller and *very* human.

Edwin flapped his wings in indignation. "You're a spy, a meddler and a snoop, just as you always were!" he said.

"I am *not!*" squeaked the weasel. He pointed his quivering pink nose towards Marnie. "I'm here to warn you and tell you that Michael's…"

There was no room for doubt now. "Is Michael dead?" Marnie asked quietly. The weasel's reply sent shivers through her soul.

"He was murdered by Toledo!"

A curious sense of calm filled the room. Now that her worst fears had finally been confirmed, Marnie felt that nothing could upset her further. But she'd forgotten one vital thing.

"What isss the warning, McTaggart?" hissed Ailsa.

"It's about Aurora! She's—"

There was a quick knock – giving the Shoebox Zoo just enough time to freeze – and Grandma peered around the bedroom door. And whatever the snowy weasel was going to say next was drowned out by Marnie's grandmother as she leapt onto a chair and let out an ear-splitting scream.

Within minutes, Gramps had the situation under control. "Calm down," he said to his trembling wife, popping the weasel into a cardboard box and taping it firmly shut. "He's out of harm's way."

"Nasty, filthy creatures," muttered Grandma. "Make sure you get on the phone to the pound right away!"

Marnie watched from a distance, biting her fingernail nervously. She had to save McTaggart. And she had to hear his warning before it was too late.

Luckily, she had the ideal opportunity to talk to Gramps alone as they drove to Kyle's party. "Do you promise you won't take him to the pound?" she pleaded. "What if nobody claims him? Maybe we could keep him…?"

Gramps looked uncertain. "I don't really know about that," he said. "He's not really ours to keep." Then he relented. "I tell you what, I promise not to do anything with our little weasel until you get back. How's that?"

Marnie nodded. But she had the horrible feeling that a vital clue may have slipped through her fingers.

CHAPTER TWELVE

COMING OF AGE

The tenpin-bowling alley echoed with cheerful noise: friends shouting encouragement to each other; the rumble of bowling balls; the scattering of pins. It was the perfect place for a cool birthday party.

Marnie curled her toes inside her plasticky bowling shoes and hugged her backpack as she scanned the hall. She breathed a sigh of relief as she spotted Kyle's familiar face and then braced herself to wade through the friends that surrounded him.

"Hey!" called Steve, a boy she knew from her old school. "We're waiting to hear all about kilts and bagpipes and stuff, and you go walking straight past." His voice was scornful and unfriendly. "Are you too good for us now, or what?"

"They probably deported her for being terminally boring," said Becky. The others chuckled.

Marnie ignored them all. There was only one person

101

she'd come to see today. "Happy birthday," she said to Kyle, unable to keep the sadness out of her voice.

"Are you OK?" he asked quietly. "You look totally out of it."

"It's been a tough day," Marnie replied. She checked to make sure no one was listening, lowering her voice as an extra precaution. Then she dropped her bombshell. "Michael Scot is dead."

"I thought he was immortal?" breathed Kyle.

But there was no time to discuss it further. "Are you just going to stand around or are we going to play?" Marnie whirled round to face an impatient Steve.

Becky was with him. "Right, me and Kyle against you and Steve," she said to Marnie, grinning innocently. "OK?"

It turned out that Marnie McBride wasn't just bad at bowling. She was spectacularly bad. Time after time, her ball rolled harmlessly into the gutter without touching a single pin. Steve was seriously unimpressed. Their opponents, on the other hand, were brilliant bowlers. And as yet another ball demolished all ten pins, Marnie found herself longing to bowl the grin right off Becky's smug face.

Inside the backpack, the Shoebox Zoo weren't having much fun either.

"We are in the midst of a battlefield!" cried Edwin, above the great thundering and crashing.

"Alwaysss ssso melodramatic," hissed Ailsa. "It'sss a

children'sss party, remember?"

Boom!

"What was *that*, then?" demanded Edwin, covering his eyes with his wings. "Does that sound like the innocent frolicking of youngsters? It sounds more like the Prussian Army!"

"We could be sliced in two by sabres, speared by lances, shot full of arrows!" Bruno groaned, his knees trembling.

Her green eyes flashing with exasperation, Ailsa wriggled to the top of the backpack and peered out, just as a bowling ball hurtled past. She ducked back inside at once. "It'sss not sssabresss and arrowsss!" she said. "It'sss the heavy artillery – cannon and cannonballsss! We musssst flee!"

Taking care to stay out of sight, they headed away from the war zone, running for their lives until—

"It's her!" shouted Bruno.

Far above them, Steve had seen *her* too. "Hey, Becky," he said. "Here's our very own TV star!"

Everyone swivelled round to look. There, perched on a stool in the corner of the bowling alley café in her crisp white suit, was Aurora Dexter.

"My mom…" said Becky, flushing with embarrassment. "She is being *so* weird."

"Don't get me wrong," said Kyle, "but was that the first time you noticed?"

Becky shrugged. "Well, now she's going to get this new show, she's gone *super-double* weird."

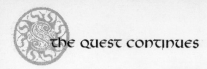

"New show?" asked Steve.

"Yeah, *Above and Beyond the Beyond*," said Becky in a thoroughly bored voice. She plugged her fingers into a bowling ball and took aim.

Marnie thought back to the last time she'd seen Aurora. It was at the Powwow, when Becky's mom had been so desperate to get the Shoebox Zoo... She gazed at Aurora – the brilliant white suit, the coiffured hair, the stark make-up. Something had changed. And that something wasn't the new TV show.

Their eyes locked. Slowly, very slowly, Aurora Dexter lifted her hand and gave the smallest of waves, sending waves of uneasiness crashing over Marnie, who tore her eyes away. Neither of them noticed that Edwin, Ailsa and Bruno picked the wrong place to hide from the bowling ball thundering towards them – behind ten pins.

Meanwhile, Marnie was having problems of her own. No matter how hard she tried to bowl – or how high, low, fast or slow – she couldn't topple more than two pins at a time. Kyle was sympathetic, throwing her encouraging smiles whenever she looked in his direction. But Steve was growing increasingly angry at her dreadful attempts, and Becky was almost hopping with glee.

And that was when Marnie heard the unmistakable voice of Juan Roberto Montoya de Toledo – his hoarse, insistent whisper drilling into her mind.

"My poor Marnie. All the power she once had is

all gone, switched off like a light. She dreams, she has visions, hears voices in her head, but she is just one of the crowd again. She has *no* power."

It was as if every part of her body had turned to lead. Marnie couldn't move a muscle. Somehow, Toledo had trapped her, was forcing her to listen to his cruel words and to witness *his* immense power.

"The great wizard Michael Scot is no more and all you have now is *me*," continued Toledo, his voice calm, hypnotic almost. "I can help you, Marnie. Look how I can help you!"

And suddenly, Marnie no longer felt rooted to the spot – quite the opposite in fact. Her body was now moving of its own accord, towards the row of bowling balls. Her fingers plunged inside the empty holes and Marnie scooped the weighty ball into the air as if it were a balloon. She ran forward and, with a gentle flick of the wrist, sent the bowling ball hurtling down the run.

"Strike!" shouted Steve, as all ten pins scattered. He clapped Marnie on the back before taking his turn.

Marnie felt dazed and totally confused. How could Toledo be controlling her like this? Where *was* he? Her skin prickled uncomfortably and, when she turned, it was no surprise to find that Aurora was still staring at her – staring with a frightening intensity. And then Marnie knew the truth… Toledo the Shapeshifter had been robbed of his body on the Day of Reckoning. And without a body, he couldn't change his shape.

So, his evil spirit had invaded the body of poor, failed psychic, Aurora Dexter.

"Come on, Marnie." Steve's hopeful words butted into her thoughts. "We need another strike to win. You can do it!"

Walk… lift ball… throw… strike. Marnie felt like just an onlooker as her limbs obeyed another. Then she heard muffled cheers and felt a glow of pride — *they'd won!* — before Toledo's seductive words seeped into her mind.

"Think of the power you could have if you had the Book," he said. "The power to return your mother to the world of the living."

Marnie badly wanted to believe. Could she *really* bring Mom back from the dead? Her eyes instinctively sought Aurora, but she'd disappeared. And at once, a terrible thought occurred to Marnie — if Aurora was Toledo, then the Shoebox Zoo was in danger! Frantically, she grabbed her backpack and peered inside. They were gone.

Blindly, she rushed towards the exit, but Kyle caught her arm. "What's up?" he asked, concern pinching his forehead.

"The Shoebox Zoo," gasped Marnie. "I think Toledo's taken them!"

"Toledo's here?"

Marnie glanced around, then lowered her voice conspiratorially. "Yeah, but something really weird's going on. It's almost like Toledo and Becky's mom are

the same person."

"Aurora's the same person as the Shapeshifter guy?" Kyle's eyebrows were so high, they were in danger of disappearing off the top of his forehead.

"*There she is!*" cried Marnie, as she glimpsed Aurora entering the ladies' toilets. Without another word, she rushed after her.

Wearing a thoroughly bemused expression, Kyle watched as the toilet door swung shut. He waited. And waited. Eventually, Aurora strode out.

With furtive glances to the left and right, Kyle backed into the toilets…

…and found himself in a deserted street. High-rise office blocks towered all around, glinting in the sun. There were no cars, no people, no Marnie. Nothing. And the door he'd just walked through had vanished. Kyle was totally alone.

Suddenly, the silence was shattered by the sound of galloping hooves and he spun round to see a white horse thundering towards him. As it pounded closer, he stared in terrified fascination at its wild eyes, huge, flared nostrils and beautiful mane rippling in the wind. It reared high above Kyle, about to crush him beneath deadly hooves when…

…Kyle was sitting by a small, crackling campfire in the middle of a misty wood. He looked around the clearing and saw his grandfather and the Shoebox Zoo. They were all watching him.

"Grandpa!" exclaimed Kyle. "And the Shoebox

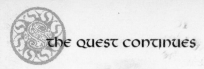

Zoo – they're safe!"

"I thought it best to bring them here," said Nathaniel. "Where were you, grandson?" he asked gently.

"I was back in Denver," said Kyle. "It was like a ghost town and there was nobody there, just me and a white horse. It was charging towards me… I thought it was going to kill me!"

Nathaniel looked relieved. "That's good," he said. "The spirits have spoken." A sudden smile sent wrinkles shooting out from the corners of his eyes and mouth. "All these years, I wasn't sure if you had the medicine in you. But today the spirits showed that you have the medicine all right – the same medicine that's inside me."

Kyle went to speak, but Nathaniel hadn't finished. "It's time you got your birthday present," he said, handing his grandson a wooden dance stick. It was a colourful little horse with a bristly mane and tail.

"Mine?" Kyle's eyes lit up and he held the dance stick reverently. "What am I supposed to do with him?"

"You could breathe life into him for a start," said Nathaniel with a chuckle.

"Me?" Kyle face crumpled. "I don't know how…"

"Sure you do," his grandfather replied. "You've got the medicine in you. Tell him, Marnie."

Marnie walked through the misty wood to the place she'd been summoned by Nathaniel. She smiled encouragingly at her best friend.

"You're OK!" said Kyle.

108

Marnie nodded, then set about trying to help. "You could concentrate," she suggested gently. "Picture him alive in your mind's eye. That's what I did with the Shoebox Zoo."

Bruno nodded.

Kyle screwed up his face in concentration, blood vessels pumping at his temples, and drew his hand across the wooden dance stick. The air shimmered magically.

"Hey, what took you so long?" Hunter whinnied, tossing back his mane and cantering around Kyle's feet.

"Happy Birthday, Kyle," said Nathaniel.

But Kyle didn't look happy – quite the opposite. And Marnie suddenly realised that even though she longed for *her* power to return, power wasn't something that Kyle wanted.

Nathaniel seemed to sense it too. "The horse medicine is wild and strong," he said gently. "You've got to learn how to ride it… And I'm getting too old to ride a horse any more. I figure *you're* ready to take over the reins."

"You mean that you want me to be you? A medicine man?" he spluttered.

"No!" said his grandfather hurriedly. "I want you to be yourself… be your own kind of Medicine Man. You're scared, Kyle. It's a heavy burden, I know."

"Sure I'm scared," said Kyle. He pointed a quivering finger at Marnie. "I've seen what happens to *her*

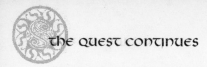

and I don't want to get that way!"

Marnie gulped. She hadn't realised how much she'd wanted Kyle's help until it seemed that he couldn't give it. Did she really have to continue this Quest on her own?

But Nathaniel wasn't about to give in. "Now, you listen to me," he said sternly. "Marnie is in great danger, which means that we're *all* in great danger. The one who was dead has come back and dead power renewed can come back *twice* as deadly, especially if it joins up with somebody living. Are you telling me that you don't want to help her?"

Kyle hung his head. "Of course I want to help her," he whispered. "Marnie's my best friend."

"Then help her to find that Book," said Nathaniel, fixing his grandson with a calm, but penetrating stare. "But you have to be willing to use the medicine that's deep inside you."

All eyes were on Kyle now, waiting for his reaction.

"I can't do this stuff…" he said. "I don't know how."

There was a collective sigh.

Nathaniel smiled sadly. "The spirits can mess up," he said. "They told me you were ready, but maybe you're not."

McTaggart the weasel had escaped from the cardboard box and scampered across downtown Denver to reach Marnie. From all the walking, his tiny paws were bloodied and swollen, but he was determined to reach her.

He wriggled through the air-conditioning vents of the bowling alley and peered inside. It seemed to be empty. "Must warn the Chosen One," he squeaked for the thousandth time. "Must warn her about Aurora…"

A dark shadow fell over him and, before he had time to flee, McTaggart was snatched by jewelled fingers. "Of course you must," said Aurora. "But not today." And she slid him into her white leather handbag.

CHAPTER THIRTEEN

THE DEAR DEPARTED

Marnie stood back from the chart that hung on her bedroom wall and examined the clues written there. "OK, so we know that Angus McBride married the daughter of Stone Bear," she said, rubbing her chin. "And we know that Angus gave *The Book of Forbidden Knowledge* to Chief Stone Bear. So what about the bear clue?"

"It's obvious!" cried Edwin from the dressing table, where he perched with Ailsa and Bruno. "How could we have been so foolish as to have missed it?"

"Missed what?" asked Marnie, without taking her eyes off the wall chart. She was too used to Edwin's outbursts by now to take much notice of them.

"The next clue, of course." The little eagle pointed his good wing at the torn page, where each of the clues had glowed. "We've had a *snake* rattle," he said, nodding smugly at Ailsa, before switching his attention to Bruno. "We've had a *bear* clue. And I am—"

"An eagle!" cried Marnie, her fingertips tingling with excitement. The only problem was, they still didn't have a clue what the eagle clue *was*, or how to follow it. The tingling in her fingertips promptly fizzled out.

"Hey!" Kyle poked his head round the bedroom door. He glanced at the chart, before turning to Marnie. "I need to talk to you," he said seriously.

Marnie was thinking far too hard about the Quest to pay attention. "We've got a bear rune and a snake rune—"

"And a horse rune," interrupted Hunter, cantering into the room. He directed a big toothy grin at Kyle and Marnie.

"Are you following me?" asked Kyle crossly.

"Yep!" replied the tiny wooden horse.

Kyle glared at him. "Don't you have somewhere else to be?"

"Nope!" He clip-clopped over to Marnie. "You dreamt of a horse rune on the plane, didn't you?" he asked.

Suddenly Marnie remembered – she *had* seen a horse. Her brain whirred into action. Just because its image had faded from the torn page didn't mean that the horse was any less of a clue than the snake rattle or bear claw.

"Marnie!"

She swung round to face Kyle. "What?"

113

"I *really* need to talk to you," he said.

There was a sharp knock at the bedroom door and only just enough time for the Shoebox Zoo to freeze before Gramps walked in. He was dressed in a cowboy outfit, with a huge, shiny belt buckle, wide Stetson and patterned cowboy boots. "Don't tell me you guys forgot about the rodeo?" he said.

And in the rush to get ready, Kyle's request was forgotten.

At the Fairmont Springs Hotel, Aurora was interrogating McTaggart the weasel, her breath clouding the glass of his prison.

"How much does Marnie know?" she demanded. "Does she know of the second prophecy? Does she know about *me*? Tell me the truth or I'll pull out your miserable whiskers one by one!"

The weasel looked up at her defiantly. "You can pull out my whiskers, skin me alive and boil me in oil for all I care. I'm telling you nothing!"

Aurora's eyes flashed with fury and she lifted McTaggart's glass case above her head as if she would smash it to pieces on the white marble floor.

"What are you doing?" cried Becky, staring at her mother in disbelief.

With a forced laugh, Aurora returned the case to the tabletop. "He's a pesky little fellow, isn't he?" she said lightly. "My goodness, he'd try the patience of a saint!"

Becky shrugged and flipped on the TV. A repeat of *Above and Beyond* was showing, complete with the old, flamboyant Aurora. Becky stared at the plasma screen wistfully.

"Watch her well," said her new, sophisticated mother. "This is your last chance. There'll be no more cable and no more Aurora. The next time you see me, you shall see the Dawn Queen!" By now, her voice had become so loud it was verging on the fanatical.

Becky looked bewildered. "The Dawn Queen?" she asked.

"Darling." Aurora crouched down so that their eyes were level. "For my new show, Aurora Dexter simply won't do. As host, I must evolve to become—" here she paused, her breathing fast and shallow, "the Dawn Queen."

But this announcement failed to excite her audience of one. "Whatever…" Becky groaned, slouching from the room.

Marnie swiftly knotted a red handkerchief around her neck and checked out her reflection in the mirror. OK, so she wasn't as dressed up as Gramps, but she'd do. There was just time to say goodbye to the Shoebox Zoo before—

"It's her!" cried Edwin, hopping wildly in front of the TV.

There, on the screen, was Aurora Dexter. She

smiled kindly at her viewers. "Here's something that someone sent in," she was saying. She opened an envelope and drew out an antique bracelet studded with green gems. "An object, something personal... A physical connection always makes it so much easier to communicate with the dear departed."

Edwin frowned, then froze as Grandma appeared in the doorway.

"Oh, good grief!" she exclaimed. "Is there no escaping that silly woman?" She turned to Marnie and smiled. "Come on, or we'll miss the start of the parade."

Marnie waited until the coast was clear before speaking sternly to the Shoebox Zoo. "OK," she said. "I want you guys to stay *right here*."

In the room below, Kyle was having equally strong words with Hunter. "No way are you coming," he hissed. "I've got to talk to Marnie and I've got to do it *alone*."

The wooden horse put his colourfully patterned head on one side. "Got something to say that you're ashamed of?"

Kyle ignored the question. "Stay here and keep an eye on the Shoebox Zoo," he said. "They listen to you. They *respect* you."

Hunter winked and leapt from the table as Marnie clattered down the stairs.

The rodeo was a seething mass of Stetsons. Suddenly,

Gramps was one of the crowd, rather than the odd one out. In the small, slightly shabby stadium, a stream of horses, cows and cowboys paraded past to the accompaniment of a marching band. Gramps and Grandma stopped to watch, but Marnie wasn't in the mood. And, it seemed, neither was Kyle.

"What's up with you?" she asked, as they walked between holding pens filled with broncos and bulls. "You're acting so weird."

Kyle hesitated. "Well, it's the whole thing, really… The Quest, the magic, Michael Scot being dead… and all that stuff my grandpa was talking about." He paused, a pained expression on his face. "It just seems like this stuff is way too serious to get mixed up in."

Marnie froze. She couldn't believe what she was hearing. "Mixed up in?" she said slowly. "I don't know if you've noticed, but I'm way past the point of just being mixed up in it." She stormed away, with Kyle hot on her heels.

"I know you need my help," he pleaded helplessly. "I want to give it, believe me."

Marnie whipped round to face him. "I don't think you do," she hissed. She was shocked by the intensity of her anger, but couldn't control it. Everyone was letting her down. First Michael, now Kyle. Why did this keep happening?

They stared at each other for a long, uncomfortable moment. Then Kyle broke the silence. "Something's changed, Marnie," he said. "You're different."

"Well, if I'm different, then you're different too," Marnie snapped. Swiftly, she changed tack. "Look, bringing Hunter to life… that's not something that just anybody can do."

Before Kyle had a chance to reply, there was a sudden commotion in an adjacent pen as a white stallion began stamping and whinnying, kicking like crazy. He shuddered as he watched.

Marnie went on with her plea regardless. "I know what power is about," she said. "I had it. I used it… Didn't you understand a word your grandpa said? We're mixed up in this thing together." Kyle said nothing – and it was obvious to Marnie that nothing she could say would make any difference. "I'm looking for a horse clue, right?" she said, totally deflated. "And if the kid with horse medicine isn't going to help me, then I guess I'm just going to have to do it on my own."

She trudged slowly away.

In Marnie's bedroom cupboard, thin shafts of light pierced the dusty shadows to reveal boxes stacked precariously on top of each other.

"What are we looking for, exactly?" Bruno's muffled voice came from the murky depths of the cupboard.

"We are looking for sssomething that belonged to Marnie'sss mother," hissed Ailsa, wriggling out of a cardboard box crammed with ancient birthday cards.

Edwin strutted to and fro on a high shelf. "Didn't you hear what Aurora said? If we have something that belonged to the dear departed soul, it'll make it easier to talk to them."

"If we find sssomething that belonged to Marnie'sss mother, ssshe can ussse it to connect with her 'dear departed' and then ssshe'll find the Book." Ailsa flicked her tongue, clearly delighted with this unarguable logic.

"You want Marnie to speak to the dead?" Bruno peered from behind a pile of books. His chocolatey eyes were filled with dread. "The dead should be left in peace..."

And that was when the Shoebox Zoo heard footsteps, creeping slowly across the bedroom floor, closer and closer, until... a little horse peeped round the cupboard door.

"What are you guys doing lurking in here?" asked Hunter curiously.

"We might ask the same question of *you*!" snapped Edwin.

Hunter flicked his tail. "Don't be smart," he said. "I could've been watching a rodeo instead of babysitting you guys."

"We have to help the Chosen One," Bruno explained sheepishly, ignoring Ailsa's long hiss of disapproval.

119

"Marnie?" said Hunter, breaking into a grin. "Well, why didn't you say so?"

Edwin stamped forward crossly, whether to tell Bruno to keep quiet or to inform Hunter that he was in charge of this investigation, no one was quite sure, because what *did* happen was that the little eagle over-balanced and tumbled from the high shelf. Down… down… down… *Crash!*

Bruno, Ailsa and Hunter peered into a box to see Edwin shaking his head woozily. He was sitting inside a padded box on top of a pile of dull beads.

"What's that?" said Hunter.

Ailsa slithered over to take a closer look, her green eyes sparkling. "Jussst the kind of thing we've been looking for," she said gleefully.

There, lying in the corner of the jewellery box, was a round silver case. An inscription was engraved in ornate lettering on its lid: *To Rosemary, on your eleventh birthday.*

Bravely, Ailsa clicked open the clasp to reveal a delicate silver bracelet nestling inside. They all peered at the bracelet, silent with awe. "I sssuggessst we put it in her drawer and then let her find it herssself," the little snake hissed. "Then we won't be to blame."

"Oh, you are ssso deviousss," said Edwin admiringly.

Bruno looked terribly unhappy. "What do you think, Hunter?" he asked, appealing to the only creature yet to speak.

Hunter shuddered dramatically. "Raising the dead?" he snorted. "The whole thing gives me the heebie-jeebies!"

CHAPTER FOURTEEN

ᏔᎥᏞᎠ ᏂᎧᎡᏕᎬᏕ

Aurora Dexter stood in the centre of Room 1111 of the Fairmont Springs Hotel. With eyes tightly shut, she raised her palms outwards and upwards, as if drawing energy from the air around her. The only sound was that of a clock, ticking relentlessly on.

Her eyelids fluttered open to reveal a dark, purposeful gaze, and Aurora lifted a silvery-white mask from its pedestal. She reverently placed it on her head.

"Give me the eyes!" she commanded, watching as…

…Marnie walked listlessly between the horse pens, trying to focus her thoughts. She hadn't a clue where Kyle was and, frankly, she didn't care. She didn't have time for quitters. If the Quest was something that she was going to have to do alone, then that was the way it had to be.

A horse harrumphed in a nearby pen and Marnie

reached across to stroke his long, smooth nose. "Are you a horse clue or are you just another horse?" she asked wearily.

"Maybe you know the answer already," was the reply, the voice strangely familiar.

Marnie stepped back in surprise. A talking weasel and now a talking horse? Was the Quest sending the whole animal kingdom crazy?

"Or maybe the clue's for somebody else."

Now Marnie saw that the horse's lips weren't moving ... She spun round to face Nathaniel. He was perched on a fence, his face grave. He was silent now, his dark eyes trapping her in their gaze.

"The clue's for Kyle?" she ventured. Nathaniel's expression brightened a little and, encouraged, she went on. "The horse clue's about Kyle and his horse medicine?" she said. She was definitely getting warm now – Nathaniel's expression told her so. Then it came to her. "The horse clue's about us working together!"

There was a great roar from the stadium and Nathaniel nodded in the direction of the crowd. "Seems like *they* think so," he said.

The laughter that rippled through Marnie was a welcome relief from the gloom that had settled upon her. But it was short-lived.

"You miss Michael, don't you?" said Nathaniel gently.

She bowed her head. Of *course* she missed Michael. He'd been with her for so long that it was hard to adjust to life without his words of encouragement, his help… and without *him*.

"He was tired and weary," Nathaniel went on. "Now, at last, he can rest."

Marnie knew this, but it didn't make the truth any easier to bear. Then, just as it seemed her spirits could sink no lower, they did.

"You miss your mom too." The words were softly spoken, but they hit Marnie like a sledgehammer. "You'd like to bring her back, wouldn't you?"

Even as tears spilled down Marnie's cheeks, she couldn't deny the flicker of hope that burned deep within her. Toledo was the last person she should trust, but his words had been *so* tempting. And to have her mother back would make her happy beyond belief.

Nathaniel had other ideas. "You know you can't bring her back, don't you?" Leaping lightly from the fence, he went to Marnie and laid a hand on her quivering shoulder. "Your mom is in the spirit world now," he said. "She's content. She's looking out for you all the time, but she can't come to you any more – even if somebody were to tell you that she can."

Reluctantly, she nodded and looked right into Nathaniel's eyes. She was surprised by the depth of emotion she saw there.

"The spirits tell me all kinds of stuff," he went on. "They told me that you had a hard road to go down – a road of shadows and loneliness. And they told me that your journey would take you through a dark mist…" He paused. "But they also told me that you weren't to worry and that soon the road would lead back into light."

"But I don't understand," said Marnie. This was too much to take in. Shadows and loneliness and dark mist?

"Marnie!"

She swung round to see Kyle running towards her, an anxious look on his face. He hung onto the fence as he caught his breath. "Who were you talking to?" he gasped.

Even as she turned to look, Marnie knew that Nathaniel would be gone. She faced Kyle, now filled with a new awareness of what he was going through. "I understand how hard it is for you," she said kindly. "The power and the horse medicine. It's really scary."

Kyle's face cleared. "My grandpa doctors people, right?" he said, words tripping over other words in the rush to explain. "He does ceremonies night after night, he helps people, he cures them too, *and* he talks to the spirits – it's like a full-time job."

Marnie listened, now realising just what Kyle was rebelling against.

"I just want to be a normal kid," he continued, his voice rising above the noise of a horse whinnying and stamping nearby. "I don't want special powers – I want to have fun; I want to go bowling, go to the ball game, get into *trouble*." He sighed heavily. "When you're a medicine man, you don't belong to yourself.

You belong to all the people who need you… and you belong to the spirits."

Kyle's words grew quieter and the rodeo disappeared from view as Marnie was thrown into another vision…

Stone Bear ran swiftly away, his fingers clenched tightly around The Book of Forbidden Knowledge… *The Native American chief looked over his shoulder, his eyes filled with terror.*

Marnie vaguely heard the sound of pounding hooves. They were drawing closer and closer. But she was powerless to run, to move even.

"Get out of the way!" cried Kyle.

At last, Marnie willed her eyelids open. She stared, transfixed, at the enormous horse thundering towards her, its powerful muscles rippling beneath a sleek, white coat. She was right in its path.

"Move, Marnie!" Kyle was becoming increasingly desperate. Any second now, Marnie would be crushed beneath the beast's hooves. And he could do nothing to save her — or could he?

Suddenly, his grandfather's voice echoed all around. "*You've got the power, Kyle… You've just got to use it.*"

He had no choice. Kyle screwed his eyes tight shut and focused his energy, directing it at the galloping horse with one trembling hand. Would it be enough?

It was.

At the very last second, the runaway horse reared into the air, snorting wildly, its deadly hooves flailing

and then landing – with the softest of thuds – just centimetres away from Marnie. She was so close that she could feel its hot breath on her face. Kyle moved past her and placed a hand on the horse's heaving flank.

"*I knew you had the medicine.*"

The horse and the rodeo vanished – and Marnie and Kyle found themselves back in misty woodland, facing Nathaniel.

"Hey, grandson," said the old man, beaming widely at Kyle. "I'm glad to see that you finally got the message." He turned to Marnie. "And maybe you ought to check that torn page of yours now."

Marnie reached into her backpack and pulled out the ancient sheet. She carefully unfolded it, then stared in wonderment at what she saw there. "The horse rune – it's back!"

"Is that because of me?" asked Kyle.

"I told you guys," his grandfather replied. "You've got to work together." He chuckled knowingly. "You have no excuse not to, seeing as you both come from the same family."

Marnie thought back to their discovery of the marriage of Stone Bear's daughter and Angus McBride. So it *was* true. She and Kyle really *were* cousins. She grinned delightedly at them both.

But Nathaniel's face was sombre. "Remember what I told you, Marnie. It's a dark road, but it will lead out into the light."

She nodded, even though she was no nearer to

understanding the ominous prediction. Mist thick-
ened and rose all around, engulfing Nathaniel and the
silvery trees. When it cleared, Marnie and Kyle were
back at the rodeo.

Things seemed different between them; better. All
remnants of their argument had faded away like the
mysterious wood.

"I've got a favour to ask you," ventured Marnie.
"I'm supposed to be going off to camp and—"

Kyle shook his head vigorously. "Singing round a
campfire? Playing pretend Indians in the wood? No
way!"

This called for emergency action. Marnie put on
her saddest expression and stared helplessly at Kyle.
"But Nathaniel just said that we were supposed to
be working together and I'm going to be all on my
own... Please?"

Kyle let out a huge sigh. "OK."

Aurora removed the mask from her head and
carefully smoothed her hair. "It looks like someone's
going camping..." she said. The laughter that followed
was long, loud and undeniably evil.

That night, Marnie found herself facing the doors
of the ancient shed once more. They creaked open
to reveal the monstrous generator inside, twin lights
flickering in the gloom like malicious eyes. Marnie
stepped forward, lured closer by an unknown force.

She watched spellbound as golden tentacles reached around the throbbing machine, stretching towards her, embracing her at last in their gleaming grip...

She wrenched herself out of the nightmare and woke up, her breathing ragged with fear. And far above, a black mist crept across the night sky to cover the full moon.

ghosts around the campfire

The next morning, Marnie found it hard to wake. She felt dreadful — her limbs heavy and tired, her mind sluggish. And when she opened her weary eyes, she saw a changed world. Sunlight was dimmer. Colours, which only the day before had been vivid, were now muted. Outside, the wind moaned dolefully. *Everything* was different.

A sharp cough caught her unawares, rattling her throat painfully, while her head throbbed so much that all she wanted to do was burrow under the duvet and slide into dreamless sleep. But a nagging thought stopped her.

Camp.

Exhausted beyond belief, she dragged her unwilling body out of bed and stared listlessly at her reflection in the mirror. Her skin was pale and her eyes appeared sunken, ringed by dark circles. Her glossy blonde hair was lank and unkempt, hanging in rats' tails. But what did she care? The only thing that mattered was the Book.

She dressed, then wrenched open her duffel bag. Impatiently tossing aside bright T-shirts and hoodies, she reached instead for her darkest clothes. Black, black and more black – clothes to suit her black mood. She coughed again.

"Are you feeling OK, pumpkin?" called Gramps.

For goodness' sake… Couldn't she get a moment's peace around here? "Give me a minute," she grumbled. "I'm still packing!"

Edwin, Ailsa and Bruno watched her warily from inside their shoebox.

"Erm, Master," began Edwin. "Oh, kind and benevolent Chosen One. You're—" His words were cut short as Marnie grabbed the shoebox and stuffed it unceremoniously inside her duffel bag.

"You can't pack usss in here like baggage!" protested Ailsa.

And at that moment, Marnie felt a welcome surge of red-hot energy flow through her. Could it be possible? Could it really be *true*? She looked desperately around the room, searching for something to… Aha! Marnie concentrated her mind and, with less effort than it takes to blink an eye, lifted the old cardboard lid into the air and slammed it on top of the shoebox, muffling the creatures' protests.

She smiled grimly. Her power was back.

Zipping the bag firmly shut and throwing it over her shoulder, Marnie made for the door. But something held her back and, without knowing why she did it, she pulled open the drawer of her dresser. There, on top of neatly paired socks, lay a silver case. It glinted dully in the pale morning light. She knew instinctively who had once owned it, even before reading the engraving: *To Rosemary, on your eleventh birthday*. Marnie flipped open the case, greedy fingers snatching the delicate bracelet inside.

Aurora Dexter's words echoed in her mind... "*An object, something personal... A physical connection always makes it so much easier to communicate with the dear departed.*"

This could be what she needed to bring her mother back to life.

Marnie headed for the door, turning back at the last moment. How could she have forgotten? She went to her bedside table and reached for the photo frame there. But she didn't look at the picture of her mother – instead, she turned it over and ran her fingers across the backing, scrabbling until a fingernail hooked open the metal clasp. The torn page lay where she'd left it, safely hidden inside the frame...

...Aurora caressed the silvery-white mask, smiling triumphantly.

"The world is full of opposites," she murmured. "True and false. Black and white. Positive and negative. It grows daily — a negative charge that flows from the Book like electricity, cancelling the positive power of the Chosen One, turning her light into darkness... and feeding *me!*"

"Mom?" said Becky, her mouth hanging open. "What are you *doing*?"

Totally unperturbed by the interruption, Aurora ran her fingers over the contours of the mask. "What peculiar things one finds in these old hotels," she said, turning to her daughter. "Mwah, mwah!" She kissed the air. "I'll miss you, darling, but you'll have such a wonderful time. And I'll be so preoccupied, getting the new show ready. This is our big break, remember?"

Becky edged away. "Sure, Mom," she said. "Whatever you say."

Her mother smiled slyly. "There's just one teensy-weensy thing you can do for me while you're at camp..."

The Shoebox Zoo creatures were worried. Very worried indeed. They paced about their cardboard home, trying to work out what was wrong with Marnie.

"It's almost like she's possessed..." said Bruno.

"Yes!" cried Edwin. "It must be some dark magic of the Shapeshifter!" He buried his beak in his wings.

"She seems to have got her powers back," Bruno added thoughtfully. "Though she doesn't seem to be using them for good."

133

"Will you two be quiet?" hissed Ailsa. "Sssomeone'sss coming!"

A door creaked open and the bag they were trapped inside was yanked into the air and dropped from what felt like a very great height.

Ooof!

Marnie saw the camp helper unloading her bag from the bus and dumping it on the ground. She angrily stormed over to claim it before more damage could be done. "Shut up!" she hissed, on hearing the frenzied babbling coming from within. "You're going to get me into trouble!"

Giggles erupted behind her and slowly she turned to see a whole crowd of children, waiting to collect their bags. They were all laughing at her, Becky most of all. Even Kyle avoided her eye – and she'd thought she could rely on *him*.

Then Gramps appeared and Marnie's heart sank still further. He looked utterly ridiculous. He was wearing khaki shorts, a shirt with the *Camp Healing Bow* logo sewn onto it, and sturdy hiking boots. Most embarrassingly of all, the outfit was topped off by a floppy canvas hat.

"How!" Gramps raised his hand and looked nervously at the young crowd. "Come along to the camp hut and we'll get you sorted."

Once inside, Marnie's eyes were drawn to the Healing Bow – the famous artefact that the camp was named after – sealed in a glass case on the wall.

She sensed its age and its power…

Soldiers advanced on Chief Stone Bear, who ran for his life, pausing only to place an arrow in the Healing Bow… A Native American ran from the scene…

Marnie snapped out of her vision as the rest of the children crowded into the camp hut, noisily scuffling for places on long wooden benches. She found a space beside Kyle.

"What's your grandpa doing here?" he asked curiously.

She hissed a reply between clenched teeth. "Don't ask me. *I* didn't invite him."

Gramps cleared his throat and the hubbub died down. "Well, folks," he began. "I'm filling in at the last moment, so if I get things muddled up from time to time, I hope you'll forgive me." He thumbed desperately through a tattered red book. "Ah… why don't we start by dividing you up into the four clans!"

Everyone tittered. Everyone, that is, except Marnie. And she had even less to laugh about when the names of the clans were announced – *Eagle, Snake, Bear* and *Wolf.*

Great. Couldn't she ever get away from the stupid Shoebox Zoo? Why did everything have to be about *them*? She felt so low, so thoroughly miserable about everything that she didn't bat an eyelid when Gramps announced that Becky and Kyle would be joining the snake clan, while she was in wolf. Deep down, she'd known it would be like this, that she would be alone.

"I know Nathaniel said we should be working together, not against each other," Kyle whispered, with an encouraging grin. "But it's just a game, right?"

Marnie scowled. "Yeah, but the Quest isn't a game, is it?" she spat back.

Kyle drew away as if he'd been scalded. "Look, you asked me to come here," he said. "So, if I can play along, so can you. Stop acting so weird. What's *with* you today, anyway?"

She didn't reply.

That evening, everyone gathered in the giant tepee. In the centre was a firepit, in which flames crackled and roared. Marnie's grandpa sat on one side of the campfire – his audience on the other.

"In honour of the Bow of Wisdom and the Arrow of Truth," Gramps said in a deep voice that Marnie recognised from storytimes when she was a child, "I share with you a tale of ghosts and spirits that walk the earth and prey on the living…"

Marnie had already had enough spirits to last a lifetime. But she was too tired to object.

"Not so very long ago, and not so very far from here," said her grandfather, "there was a graveyard, and there was a girl… This girl argued with her friends and, as the sun set, she walked home alone through the graveyard. And although the girl wasn't afraid of ghosts, she had to admit that the graveyard was a lot scarier in the dark than it was by daylight…"

A semi-circle of captivated faces watched, lit by the spooky glow of the fire. Only Becky was bored. "Ghost stories? How old are we?" she scoffed. "Is this guy for real?"

"Are you scared, Becky?" Marnie said slyly.

"As if!" Becky spluttered. "I'm out of here." And, quickly slipping through a gap in the tepee, she went.

"Her friends could no longer see her though the deepening shadows," Gramps went on. "And when she turned around, she could no longer see them. She was all alone…"

Marnie knew just how the girl felt.

Inside Marnie's cabin, the Shoebox Zoo creatures had escaped again. With a great deal of cunning – plus a lot of jiggling and jumping – they'd eventually freed themselves from the shoebox and the backpack. They were recovering from their exertions when the doorknob turned and, with a dreadful creaking of unoiled hinges, the wooden door slowly swung open. Quivering with trepidation, they watched from beneath a bunkbed as a dark figure crept into the cabin.

"It'sss her!" hissed Ailsa. "Aurora'sss daughter!"

Becky tiptoed inside and, with a wicked chuckle, headed straight for Marnie's backpack. She tugged the zip open and then began rifling through the contents. "So you think you can make me look dumb, Marnie McBride?" she muttered. "I'll show you! Now,

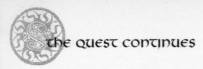

where's that stupid piece of paper?"

"She's after the torn page!" squeaked Edwin.

Bruno flexed his stone muscles. "We must stop her!" he said. He quickly explained his plan to Ailsa and Edwin, before ambling away.

"Gotcha!" exclaimed Becky, triumphantly waving her prize.

Suddenly, a bright circle of light appeared on the wall beside her, the terrifying silhouette of a huge bear at its centre.

"Thief!" squawked a terrible voice. "Yes, *you*! You should never probe into what is not yours. Begone! Wooooo!" The monster's arms waved menacingly above its grotesque head.

Becky didn't argue. She dropped the page and bolted.

Edwin and Ailsa could hardly lower the flashlight to the ground, they were laughing so much. Bruno jumped down from the bunk to join them – a tiny bear who had created an enormous shadow by using a trick of the torchlight.

Gramps was winding up his ghostly tale as Becky crept back inside the tepee, shaking with fear. "Now, the girl was filled with a terrible terror," he said. "And she screamed. Arggghhhh!"

"*Arggghhhh!*" screamed his audience – Becky louder than the rest, Marnie less than most.

"And when they found her the next morning, she

was dead," Gramps said. He paused dramatically. "So, was it a ghost or was it fear? Because our fears can hurt us as badly as a real ghost..."

At that moment, a sudden gust of wind blew through the tepee, snuffing out the fire and plunging everyone into blackness.

Marnie felt strangely at home in the dark.

CHAPTER SIXTEEN

A DARK DEED

At daybreak, Kyle sneaked out of his cabin and hurried deep into the woods, where he wouldn't be disturbed. Once safely hidden from sight, he took the wooden horse from his pocket and placed it carefully on the ground. He closed his eyes in concentration, then passed his hand over the dancestick.

The air shimmered and the little horse came alive, stretching and whinnying with delight. "I am Sunkwaki, Spirit— Mm mmph." His traditional greeting was stifled as fingers clamped over Hunter's muzzle.

"Shhhh!" Kyle whispered. "I know who you are. You don't have to do that whole I-am-this-and-that-and-the-other routine every time, OK?"

Hunter nodded reluctantly, but perked up at his master's next words.

"I need you to get a message to my grandpa," Kyle said. "And I'm in a real hurry, OK?"

The little horse nodded his head so vigorously that it was surprising it didn't fly off. Then he obediently galloped away.

Becky slept soundly, her cheek squished into the pillow and one arm dangling over the side of her bunk. Above her, the tiny window squeaked open a couple of centimetres and the end of a pipe wriggled, snakelike, through the gap.

"Ha!" said Edwin from his vantage point on top of the hose. "This will teach the ungracious brat to steal from the Chosen One."

Ailsa nodded in agreement. "Revenge isss ssssweet," she hissed.

They turned to give Bruno the signal and – *Whoosh!* – a torrent of water gushed out, splashing onto Becky's head.

Stopping only to grab a bucket filled to the brim with last night's washing-up water, Becky stomped towards Marnie's cabin to confront her. They met on the steps, where Marnie was rubbing sleep from her eyes.

"You think you're so smart, Princess Plays-with-baby-toys!" Becky roared as water dripped off her nose. She was too angry to notice the water slopping onto her slippers.

"What are you talking about?" Marnie said groggily. She was oblivious to the Shoebox Zoo's antics since they'd arrived at camp – and no wonder. They might

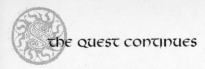

be looking out for her, but they were far too scared to talk to her.

"Like you don't know!" said Becky. She pulled back her arm and swung the bucket in a wide arc towards her target.

Marnie instantly heard the sound of rushing blood in her ears. She was livid. How *dare* an insignificant little worm like Becky treat her like this? She'd done *nothing* to deserve it. She focused all her power into a single sizzling look and – to the astonishment of the crowd that had gathered around them – instead of drenching Marnie, Becky swung the bucket up, up, up… and tipped it over her own already-soaking head.

Laughter erupted all around.

Five minutes' later, the accused sat in a single, forlorn line on the bunk. Guilt was written all over their faces as they stared at Marnie – their judge *and* jury.

"We–we–we caught her trying to steal the torn page," explained Edwin. "We–we–we thought we should teach her a lesson."

Marnie frowned at them, unsure what was truth and what was lies. The Shoebox Zoo had never been terribly good at telling the truth, after all. She reached inside her pocket and pulled out her mother's bracelet, dangling it in front of their anxious faces. "And you wouldn't happen to know how this got into my bedroom drawer, would you?" she asked.

In perfect unison, all three shook their heads.

Marnie held them in her steely gaze a moment longer before sentencing them. "Fine," she said. "If I still can't trusssst you, you'd better come with me."

Hunter had galloped long and hard, through forests, over mountains and across raging rivers – well, one rather lively stream, anyway. Now he'd reached his destination.

He delivered a message punctuated by gasps for breath. "I bring… an urgent message… from your… grandson—"

"He's worried about Marnie," said Nathaniel. "I know."

Hunter's wooden shoulders sank, as if all the oomph had seeped out of him.

"You did well to come," Nathaniel reassured him. "You can have a ride back with me."

Back at camp, Gramps was announcing the day's activity. "Now, some of you are predators," he said. "Others are prey. Prey animals get points by find-ing marked sources of food and water, and predators get points for catching prey. All of you prey animals, try to stay out of sight of any predators who might catch you." As he talked, he walked around the group, dispensing handwritten cards to everyone.

Delighted and not-so-delighted cries echoed around the camp.

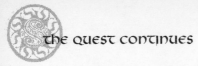

"Oh no… a mouse?"

"Yes! Eagle!"

"Chipmunk?" Marnie sighed. She might have guessed she'd be one of the hunted. She glanced up as Kyle received his card.

"Horned owl – cool!"

Gramps finished his jaunty briefing, clearly getting into the swing of camp life now. "Prey animals, you get a five-minute head start to find some food, water and shelter, OK? Go!"

Marnie headed for the deepest, darkest part of the wood, where a low mist floated above the ground and only the barest amount of sunlight filtered down through the trees. With narrowed eyes, she peered into a small, gloomy clearing.

"Where are we and what are we doing?" Edwin's prim voice sounded deafening in the stillness.

Then Gramps' voice could be heard in the distance. "Predators, be off! Let the hunt begin!" The announcement was followed by faint whoops and yells.

"Who are thessse predatorsss that are after usss?" hissed Ailsa.

Marnie grabbed the backpack and whispered angrily into it. "Will you shut up!"

Too late. Becky crept between the trees, searching for a somewhere to hide. "Who were you talking to?" she asked, her voice echoing across the clearing.

Instantly, Marnie sensed a weakness in her. Whether it was because the girl was separated from the others or because of the wicked pranks the Shoebox Zoo had played on her, she couldn't be sure. But now was the time to pounce. "I was talking to a ghost, of course..." she said.

"You know what?" said Becky, backing away. "I'm just going to let some predator catch me. It'll be better than hanging around with *you*."

Marnie smiled menacingly and half-closed her eyes, allowing the dark power to flow through her once more. She concentrated hard, summoning an eerie wind – it swirled round and round, circling the clearing and cutting them off from everyone else.

"What's going on?" asked Becky, really scared now.

"It's the ghosts," murmured Marnie. "They're all around you. Can't you feel them?" She suppressed a laugh. Becky was convinced, totally. "It's the spirits – like the ones your mom talks to. She said something on her show the other day."

"She says a lot of weird things," whispered Becky.

"No, I actually *believe* this one," said Marnie seriously. "She said it was easier to speak to the 'dear departed' if you had something that *belonged* to them." She slid her hand into her pocket and pulled out the silver bracelet. "It was my mother's," she said. "I could use it to talk to her – that's what your mom said."

"I d–d–don't think you can believe everything she says," Becky stammered.

145

But Marnie wasn't listening any more. Out of the corner of her eye, she saw a black feathery heap lying on the grass. It was a dead blackbird. Evil surged inside her once more as…

The generator rattled and shook as if it were alive… The Book of Forbidden Knowledge *appeared before it, whirling like a spinning top…*

Hardly aware of what she was doing, Marnie knelt down beside the dead bird. She was no longer in control of the dark force – it was controlling her.

The Shoebox Zoo crept out of the backpack and watched in horror as Marnie spread her arms wide, palms towards the sky. She directed her gaze at the blackbird, her concentration evident by the pulsing veins at her temples. Her whole body shook violently and then stopped. Then, strangely calm, Marnie touched the bird and a zap of energy passed from fingers to feathers. Slowly, unbelievably, one amber eye opened. It was just the signal Marnie needed. She picked up the blackbird, which fluttered its wings and cawed weakly. It was *alive*.

This was too much for Becky. She swayed like a tree on a windy day and then fell. She was out cold.

"You can't do this!" cried Bruno. "You mustn't!"

"Ssshe mussst!" said Ailsa. "If ssshe'sss to contact her mother and locate the Book!"

But nothing could interrupt Marnie now. She tossed the blackbird into the air, where it barely flapped its wings before dropping to the ground like a stone. There, it blinked twice before its eyes closed again. It was dead once more.

Bruno looked sickened by what he'd seen. "The dark magic of life and death are not to be trifled with," he said.

His words filtered into Marnie's tired mind. She turned on the little bear. "So you don't care if I contact my mother or not?" she said in a low voice. "Would you rather spend the rest of your life as a lump of rock?"

Bruno's eyes were solemn. "If this black magic is what it takes to free me," he said, "then I'd gladly stay a rock."

"Fine," said Marnie. She could do without interfering do-gooders. "Have it your way." With that, she gathered all her strength, then grasped Bruno and slammed him into a rock. He instantly became imbedded in its solid face. Unrepentant, she glared at the little bear, totally still apart from his soft, brown eyes. "At least I won't have to listen to your whining any more," she said, before a coughing fit wracked her body with pain.

Marnie became aware of a pitiful noise coming from nearby. Becky had buried her head in her lap and was sobbing uncontrollably. And as she watched, Marnie felt a slow remorse trickling through her body, cooling the hot anger that had taken hold of her. She felt different – calmer, happier, almost light-hearted with relief that the darkness had receded, and revolted at the way she'd treated Becky. "Are you all right?" she asked, helping Becky to her feet. "I'll take you to sick bay."

"Thanks," Becky said doubtfully.

Bruno was long forgotten. Sadly, he watched them leave.

Aurora Dexter was in a devilishly bad mood. With the far-reaching vision that the mask gave her, she'd watched Marnie and Becky make their way back through the wood. Together.

"Stupid child!" she screamed, tearing the mask from her head. "If she makes friends with the Chosen One, the torn page will never be mine."

McTaggart, who had taken to racing round his glass prison in never-ending circles while formulating his next escape plan, skidded to a halt. "You're a cheat and a bully and a liar!" he squealed. "You're a shapeshifting trickster without an ounce of common decency in you! How can you attack a poor, defenceless child who's already lost her mother?"

At this, a wonderful smile spread across Aurora's face. "But she does have a father," she murmured. "And a father without a mother is very lonely indeed." She snapped her fingers. "The father is the key to the child – and the child will lead me to the Book!"

CHAPTER SEVENTEEN

SPIRITED AWAY

By that evening, Marnie's black mood had returned. Desperate to escape the pointless chatter of the girls in her cabin, she'd come to the empty dining hall to think. But Gramps had found her.

"Becky's going to be in sick bay until tomorrow at least," he said, frowning. "What *happened* between you two out there in the woods?"

Marnie's explanation was brief and unapologetic. "The 'predator and prey' thing freaked her out." She coughed loudly – by now her throat felt as if she'd swallowed razor blades – and noticed Gramps' worried expression. "I just don't feel well," she mumbled.

"Are you missing your father?" he asked gently. "He's going to be here soon. Honey, I know it's a bit difficult having your old grandpa at camp with you, but it's not so bad, is it? It's kind of nice spending time together."

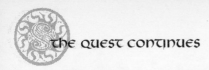

Marnie was no longer listening, her eyes drifting towards the bow suspended in the glass case on the wall...

The Book of Forbidden Knowledge *spun slowly in mid-air... Aurora Dexter reached out her hands. The Book is mine! she shouted... Chief Stone Bear examined the Arrow of Truth carefully... And Wolfgang's voice echoed within the vision: The Bow of Wisdom and the Arrow of Truth...*

"Marnie?" At the sound of Gramps' voice, the vision cleared. "Are you all right?"

"I'm tired," she said, struggling to her feet. "I think I'll go to bed." Marnie badly needed time to think – to sort through the jumbled images of her vision. As she snatched up her backpack, a small, metal creature tumbled out and crashed to the floor. She reached down, but Gramps got there first – and in a brief tug-of-war, poor Edwin's wing was ripped off.

"I'm sorry," said Gramps.

Trying not to show how angry she felt, Marnie stuffed the damaged wing back into its socket. "It's no big deal," she muttered and hurried from the room.

The cabin was dark when she returned. The only sounds were soft snuffles and snores from sleeping girls. As silently as a prowling wolf, Marnie made her way to her bunk, where she reached under her pillow and pulled out the precious picture of her mother. Briefly pausing to look at the photo, she flipped the frame over and removed the backing. But she needn't have worried – the torn page was still intact.

Ailsa slunk out of the backpack. "What isss it?" she hissed.

Edwin was right behind her. He looked nervously up at Marnie.

"You were right, Eddie," whispered Marnie. "It's the eagle rune." Sure enough, an eagle now glowed on the page alongside the other vital clues – a snake, a bear and a horse.

Mr McBride glared at the carousel that was stubbornly refusing to give up his luggage and yawned widely. When, at last, his suitcase appeared, he quickly claimed it before making his way through customs and then out into Denver International Airport.

His steps slowed at the arrivals gate. A woman waited there. She was dressed in an immaculate white suit, dark red hair swept back from her beautifully made-up face. But her outfit wasn't nearly as remarkable as the large name card she was holding up. Upon it, in large, ornate letters were the words: ROSS McBRIDE.

"Ross, there you are," said the woman, a smile perfectly outlined in scarlet softening her hard features. "How was your flight?"

"I didn't expect anyone to be picking me up," he replied, ignoring her question.

"Picking you up?" The woman giggled. "Oh, that would be *highly* inappropriate."

"Oh, no. What I meant was..." Mr McBride flushed

to the roots of his sandy hair. But before he could protest further, the woman had grabbed his suitcase – she seemed surprisingly strong – and was ushering him towards the exit. "This is extremely kind of you," he said anxiously. "I'll tell you where I'm going."

She put a finger to her lips. "Don't worry," she said. "I know *exactly* where we're going."

A few minutes later, they were cruising down a deserted downtown street in the back of an exceedingly long and dazzlingly white limousine.

"You don't remember me, do you?" asked Aurora gently. "I'm Becky's mother. She and Marnie went to school together."

Ross McBride shifted uncomfortably in his seat. "Sorry, I didn't recognise you," he said.

Aurora shrugged to show that it didn't matter a jot. "I've had something of a makeover," she explained. "I have a show on Channel 411. Rosemary's father used to work for me... Didn't he say I'd be meeting you at the airport?"

"No..." His voice trailed off, as he seemed to realise something. "You knew my wife," he said simply.

This was the signal that his travelling companion had been waiting for. In one fluid movement, she reached over and took Ross's hand, giving it a sympathetic squeeze. "I'm *so* sorry," she said. "It must have been terrible for you... and for Marnie."

"Er..." Ross tried to pull his hand away, but Aurora had a vice-like grip. "Grandma – Dorothy, that is – is

expecting me," he said quickly.

Aurora's response was quicker. "She said she'd be out all day. I think she was hoping that *I* would entertain you." Her eyelashes fluttered like frantic spiders' legs.

The charm offensive was working at last. Ross McBride sank back into the luxurious leather seat and smiled awkwardly at Aurora, who directed her penetrating gaze right back at him. At once, he was asleep.

Casually, she flipped open her mobile phone and tapped in a number. "Hello?" she said. But her sophisticated drawl had changed into a lilting Scottish voice – Ross McBride's voice. "Dorothy, I'm so sorry," she said huskily. "I've been unexpectedly detained for a few days… No, don't worry. I'll make it in time to see Marnie at camp." She snapped the phone shut and pointed one elegant finger at the snoozing passenger.

"Wh–wh–whassup?" mumbled Mr McBride, starting awake. His eyes darted around the plush, white interior of the limousine before coming to rest on the woman in the white suit, who was now brandishing a bottle of red wine. "I must have dozed off," he said. "I'm so sorr—"

Pop! Aurora pulled the cork from the bottle and glugged a generous amount of wine into a large wineglass. She handed this to Mr McBride and then filled another for herself. "Here's to daughters!" she said, clinking her glass against his.

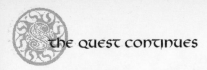

"Daughters…" Marnie's dad replied, taking a tentative sip.

Aurora leaned towards him. "I know what it's like trying to raise a daughter all by yourself," she murmured. "It must be hard for you, a single father. You must be lonely…"

"Well, sometimes." Mr McBride reddened and fiddled with his napkin.

"But so *proud* of Marnie," continued Aurora.

"I am," said Mr McBride, nodding vigorously. "But what she really needs now, more than ever, is her mother. And that's the one thing I can't give her."

She took his hand and looked deep into his eyes. "No, but you can introduce her to a positive female role model," she said, smiling. Then she gave a little gasp, as if an idea had just occurred to her. "Hey, why don't we surprise the girls? We could go to camp together for Parents' Day!"

Marnie's dad tugged his hand away. "I don't know about that," he said. "I haven't seen Marnie for weeks."

"All the more reason!" Aurora's eyes were flashing with excitement now. "It'll be fun, trust me. I was an eleven-year-old girl myself once."

Ignoring Ross McBride's concerned expression, she cupped her hands secretively around her shiny wineglass and smiled. A dark-red reflection of Toledo the Shapeshifter leered back at her.

Marnie sat in a lonely corner of the dining hut, toying with her porridge and listening to the rain thrumming relentlessly on the wooden roof. She had hardly slept, she'd been so busy thinking about the clues on the torn page. Now, dark circles hung beneath her eyes and her cough was worse than ever. She'd never dreamt that the Quest would make her feel this terrible.

A tray clattered onto the table. She looked up crossly as Kyle thumped down into the chair opposite her. "Where's Bruno?" he demanded. Then, without waiting for a reply, "You left him out there in the woods, inside a rock!"

Marnie wondered vaguely who had told him – Edwin, she supposed. She made a mental note to interrogate the traitorous eagle later.

"What's your problem?" Kyle continued, his face wearing a look of utter confusion. "One minute you're begging me to help you with this stupid Quest – and the next, you're totally mean!"

Marnie coughed painfully. "I never begged," she said.

Kyle's expression softened. "Are you sick or something?" he asked. "Look at you. Your clothes, your hair…"

Marnie snapped back, "Well, maybe I don't want to be like Becky!"

"Why are you being like this?" Kyle said. "Why were you so nasty to Becky?"

And suddenly, Marnie realised that even she didn't

know why she was acting this way, why she felt so down or even who she *was*. Then darkness pushed out doubt. "It's not my fault that Becky's chicken," she muttered. "And she hasn't exactly been nice to me, right?"

There was no response from Kyle, just a look of disappointment.

"Look, why don't you go and help poor little Becky?" Marnie said coldly. "I've got an arrow to find." She rose stiffly to her feet and stalked away. She wanted to be alone.

Gramps waylaid her as she marched across the camp. "Wait!" he called. "I've got something to cheer you up!" He put a hand in his pocket and drew out a little eagle. Its wobbly, old wing was now securely attached and its metal body had been polished until it shone.

Marnie hardly recognised the cheery voice that burst from her. "Oh, Gramps!" she cried. "You fixed him!"

For a moment, she felt truly happy. Then, as she watched the rain splashing all around them, she remembered Bruno and thought how cold and wet he must be, trapped in his rocky prison.

CHAPTER EIGHTEEN

The Eagle has Landed

Thunder boomed overhead as a deluge of rain tumbled onto the camp, bouncing off roofs and lashing against windows, turning the dry ground into a sea of mud. Everyone was sheltering inside the largest hut, where Marnie's grandpa's instructions were almost drowned out by the deafening noise of the wild weather.

"Welcome to 'Wilderness Survival'!" he shouted across the crowded room. "I'll be pairing you up and putting your orienteering skills to the test. Once your partner has been assigned, you mustn't leave their side for any reason." He looked sternly about the group, pinpointing Marnie with his stare. "OK?"

Marnie pushed lank hair out of her eyes and tried to smile back at Gramps. But inside, she was seething. What was *with* the never-ending group activities? Why couldn't people just leave her alone?

"All right," continued Gramps. "Nicole, I'll team you up with… Hannah. Brendan and Alex. Kyle…"

No, no, *no*! Marnie held her breath, willing her grandpa to pick someone else.

"…and Marnie."

She sighed heavily and glanced across the room, catching Kyle's eye. He didn't look exactly thrilled at the announcement either. Thank goodness for rain. If this downpour continued, there wasn't any likelihood of an orienteering exercise.

The rain stopped.

Gramps beamed. "Collect your gear, guys," he said brightly. "It looks like the weather is on our side after all!"

Without a word to anyone, Marnie followed in the wake of eager orienteers, squelching over muddy ground towards her cabin.

Sadly, Kyle watched her go before heading in the opposite direction towards his own sleeping quarters. And, on his bunk, there was a surprise waiting for him in the shape of a little wooden horse.

"Hunter! What are you doing?" he whispered. "Somebody will *see* you!"

"Hey, don't get cranky with me!" the little horse said, pawing the blanket crossly. "*You're* the one who sent me to find Nathaniel."

Quickly, Kyle knelt by the bunk, shielding Hunter with his jacket, so no one else could see. "So, what did Grandpa say?" he asked.

Hunter gave a delighted whinny. "Loads of stuff!" he announced. "He said that no matter what happens, you've got to stick by Marnie."

"Yeah, right," said Kyle, his face glum.

"You've got to stick by her even if she seems like a different person," insisted Hunter. "Even if she does something *really* bad."

"Like what?" asked Kyle.

"Er… he didn't say, exactly." The little horse frowned. "But she's on her own path. *Everyone's* got their own path to follow, OK? You've got *your* path and no one can walk it for you, not even your grandpa." His next words settled it. "Marnie's path affects all of us. If she strays too far into the fog, we're all lost – for good!"

Much to Marnie's dismay, when she set out from camp, Kyle was at her side.

"I don't have time to do this 'wilderness' thing," she said, through gritted teeth. "I have to find the eagle clue, the Arrow of Truth. So, if you're not going to help, there's no point you coming."

Kyle's reply was the last thing she expected. "I'll help you," he said. "But on one condition."

She came to an abrupt halt and looked warily at him.

"When we find the arrow," Kyle said, "you let Bruno out of the rock."

Anger burned deep within Marnie. How *dare* he

tell her what to do. *She* was the Chosen One, not him. But then the fight went out of her and she wondered if, perhaps, it would be a good idea to have some help. She was so tired, after all…

"OK," she said.

"Time's a-wasting!" Hunter shouted cheerily, swatting flies with his bristly tail. "You'd better find the eagle clue before you lose *another* day bickering!"

Edwin poked his head out of Marnie's backpack and then hopped to the ground. "And where exactly are we supposed to find an eagle?" he said, spreading his wings wide. "I see trees, I see rocks, I see mountains, but I don't see any eagles!"

Marnie felt a tingle of excitement run through her. How could she have been so dumb? She looked at Kyle and knew that he was thinking exactly the same thing. "*You're* an eagle, Edwin!" she cried.

Thoughtfully, Edwin put his head on one side. Then he opened his beak and squawked, "I am *not* an eagle! I am Edwin de Wynter, top-class student and grade A apprentice to the great wizard Michael Scot!"

"Well, right now, you're the closest thing we've got to an eagle," said Kyle matter-of-factly. "How well can you fly?"

"*Fly?*" screeched Edwin. "Don't be ridiculous. I can't *fly!*"

"But Gramps fixed your wing," Marnie reminded him.

Ailsa slithered out of the backpack and into

Marnie's top pocket. "That'sss all he'sss been talking about all day," she said.

Excuses spouted from Edwin faster than water from a burst pipe. "But that doesn't mean I'm aerodynamically proficient yet. It takes years of practice and a keen sense of thermal resistance. Don't you need a licence for that sort of thing?"

It was Kyle who solved the problem. He stooped down and quickly plucked a pure white feather from the ground. "See this feather?" he said, waving it under Edwin's nose. "It's been in my family for six generations. "It was given to my ancestors by the Great Eagle. It's got *heap big magic*. And if you hold it, you'll be able to fly."

Marnie's suspicions vanished as she realised what Kyle was up to. "But first you need the Dance of Power," she said. "Come on, Kyle. The Dance of Power?"

"The Dance of Power…" murmured Kyle. For a moment, he looked totally blank and then he flashed Marnie a mischievous look and began to dance.

Moving slowly at first, Kyle's dance became more and more dramatic, as he ducked, leapt, punched the air and, finally, spun on the spot. It was perfect. Marnie had to cross her arms tightly to stop herself applauding.

"Good heavens," breathed Edwin, clutching the feather. "I felt it move, almost as if it were alive with the spirit of your ancestors."

"See?" said Kyle. "You *can* fly. Just hop on Hunter's back." And he scooped up Edwin, plonking him unceremoniously on the multicoloured horse's back.

"I am not going anywhere in this most undignified position!" squawked Edwin. "I demand that you let me go—"

Too late. Hunter was already galloping through the trees at top speed, with Edwin bouncing and jolting at every step, clinging onto the horse and the white feather for dear life. "This is not funny!" he screeched.

Marnie watched them go, but her smiles turned to frowns as she realised which way the tiny duo were heading.

"Look out!" cried Edwin as the ground in front of them seemed to just... run out.

Hunter ignored him and speeded up, racing towards the cliff edge as if it were the finishing post of a great race, faster and faster until, with a clatter of wooden hooves, he came to a dead stop, catapulting Edwin high over his head and into the empty beyond.

"Arrrrgggghhh!" cried Edwin, dropping like a stone.

Far above, Marnie had reached the dizzying edge and was peering down anxiously, fear tying her stomach into knots. "Spread your wings!" she called. She knew Edwin could do it. The question was: *would* he?

"You have the feather!" shouted Kyle.

"Just *fly!*" cried Hunter.

Marnie watched, mesmerised, as the fragile metal eagle hurtled towards the raging river at the foot of the cliff. He plummeted down, down, down towards the swirling torrent and jagged rocks and what, by now, must be certain death. Until…

Whoosh! At the very last second, and for the first time in eleven hundred years, Edwin spread his wings wide and flew up and out of the chasm. "Woooooo! Look at me!" he called. "I. Am. Fantastic!"

Her eyes prickling with happy tears, Marnie watched Edwin glide round in a majestic, sweeping circle above her head, still clutching the precious feather. "Are you ready to be our spy plane?" she shouted.

A faint reply fluttered downwards. "At your service!"

The great chase began. As Edwin swooped and soared high above the treetops, Marnie and Kyle tried to keep up with him at ground level, stumbling through undergrowth, splashing through streams and trying to dodge trees before they ran into them – not easy, when their eyes were fixed firmly on the skies. And, just when they'd almost run out of oomph, Edwin spotted something – a big, feathery something with *very* wide wings.

"I can see an eagle!" he cried.

It was not just any old eagle, but a magnificent bald eagle, its black and white plumage visible from far below. Marnie felt her pulse quicken. They were getting closer – she could feel it.

"I can see an eagle's nest!" cried Edwin. And, by the simple means of pulling in his wings, he fell straight into it.

"The eagle has landed," observed Hunter.

Marnie squinted upwards. "Edwin, are you OK?" she called.

"OK? I am rather more than OK!" came the reply. "I have found the arrow!"

But so, it seemed, had the bald eagle. "Watch out!" cried Kyle, as the bird of prey zoomed closer to protect its nest.

Edwin lunged at the ancient arrow that was wedged inside the mass of twigs that made up the nest. He tugged hard, feeling it shift and then – *twang!* – it came loose just as the nest darkened under the shadow of the approaching eagle. Edwin desperately threw himself over the side and plummeted towards the ground. But in his eagerness to grab the arrow, he'd lost his feather.

"Oh, no!" he cried. "I've lost the feather!"

"Forget the feather!" called Marnie. "You don't need it!"

"Jussst fly, you sssilly bird!" hissed Ailsa.

And Edwin did. He spread his wings wide and flew – without the feather and without fear. He rode the air currents, then dipped and soared towards Marnie and Kyle, the arrow held firmly in his metal talons.

Marnie reached out for him, but at the last moment, Edwin dropped the arrow into Kyle's waiting hands instead. "Hey, that's mine!" she said.

But Kyle wouldn't budge. "I'll keep it safe until you release Bruno," he said.

Instantly, the darkness that Marnie had held at bay was back with a vengeance. She turned on her heel and stomped angrily away.

Edwin fluttered up to Kyle's shoulder. "That was some heap big magic in that feather," said the little metal bird.

"It was just an old feather," said Kyle with a chuckle.

Hunter nodded his patterned head. "Looks like you learned to fly all on your own, buddy!"

Meanwhile, Marnie had reached for the clearing where she'd imprisoned Bruno. She didn't see why she should free the traitorous bear in order to claim what was rightfully hers, but if that was what it took... She forged on, muttering in disbelief at how Edwin had taken Kyle's side. It now seemed that Ailsa was her only ally.

She looked down at the forest floor, but where the rock had lain, there was now just a small hollow.

"He's gone!" she gasped.

CHAPTER NINETEEN

A SHOCKING REVELATION

I f Marnie's days were becoming nightmarish, her nights were even worse. Now, it seemed that all she had to do was close her eyes for the torment to begin. Night after night, she relived the appalling dream – if it *had been* a dream – where she'd approached the generator shed and the throbbing, rattling machine within, and where the golden tentacles had reached for her, holding her tightly in their evil grip. And always, she heard Wolfgang's voice warning her: "No, Marnie... Don't go in there... You mustn't go in there."

Tonight was no exception. As terrifying images snaked through her subconscious, Marnie thrashed wildly, sweat beading her forehead. "No! I won't go in there!" she cried aloud, waking the sleepers all around.

A few girls nervously approached Marnie's bunk. "Shouldn't we go and get somebody?" one of them whispered, while another flipped on the light switch. But the bulb flickered and dimmed, while outside, sparks crackled and leapt along the electricity wires.

"Get away from me!" shouted Marnie, as she was pulled towards the generator once more. "Don't come near me!" With a terrible scream, she lurched awake from her nightmare, to find herself surrounded by a sea of anxious faces.

The next day was the last day of camp. Marnie skipped breakfast – she was too tired and miserable to cope with the nervous looks that everyone was sending her way. Instead, she spent the time packing her belongings, busily thinking of ways to seize the Arrow of Truth from Kyle.

When she was done, Marnie lugged her bags to the front of the main hut, ignoring Ailsa's hisses of disapproval at the bumpiness of the journey. She stopped dead when she saw Kyle and Becky chatting together on the front steps.

"Sorry," said Becky, not sounding sorry at all. "This is a freak-free zone."

"Seen any ghosts in sick bay?" retorted Marnie, laughing mirthlessly when Becky scrambled to her feet and hurried away.

Kyle wasn't amused. "Why do you have to be so *mean* to her?" he said angrily.

Marnie didn't bother to reply. "I need the arrow," she said.

"Did you get Bruno out of the rock?" Kyle asked.

She hesitated. "Well, I was going to," she said, aware even as she spoke that her reply must sound highly suspect, "but he's gone."

"That's kind of convenient." He folded his arms and, for the first time ever, looked truly disappointed in her.

Marnie didn't have time for this. She needed the Arrow of Truth and, whatever it took, she was going to get it. "Give me the arrow," she hissed, the words whistling through clenched teeth. "I'm the Chosen One, not you."

Kyle didn't budge. If anything, he looked more determined than ever not to give it to her.

As her anger increased, Marnie felt the dark power rising within her. "You don't want to see me mad, OK?" she growled, and their eyes locked in a savage battle of wills. Then, suddenly, she felt large hands grasp her shoulders and her arms flailed wildly in a desperate attempt to get away.

"Whoa, steady there!" said a familiar voice.

Marnie jerked her head back and glared at her assailant, who grinned right back at her.

"You're looking a little peaky, sweetheart," her father said softly. "And what's with the new look?" He held his arms wide.

Marnie flung herself at him. "I'm fine, Dad," she whispered, weak with relief. "As long as you're here, I'll be fine."

"I hadn't realised how much you two look alike."

The words were softly spoken and utterly charming, but they cut Marnie to the quick. She pulled herself away from her father and stared in growing horror at the woman in the white suit who stood beside him. But worse was to come. Aurora Dexter stepped forward and gripped Mr McBride's hand with her own.

"Dad!" gasped Marnie. "What are you doing?"

Quickly, he untangled his fingers. "You remember Aurora, don't you?" Mr McBride said nervously. "Becky's mother?"

Aurora smiled graciously and extended a white-gloved hand towards Marnie, who swiftly folded her arms in protest. The woman might be able to fool everyone else, but Marnie wasn't about to fall for her act.

"Mom!" shouted Becky, hurrying over.

Aurora held her daughter at arm's length. "Darling," she said, calmly planting a couple of kisses in mid-air.

"Why are you being so rude?" Marnie's dad whispered to her. "What's wrong with you?"

How could she even begin to explain that Aurora's body had been taken over by an evil force; that Aurora was trying to snatch *The Book of Forbidden Knowledge* from her; that Aurora simply wasn't Mom. "I—I don't trust her," she said meekly.

"Don't be ridiculous," said Dad. "You don't know her!"

Aurora grasped his arm possessively. "Becky,"

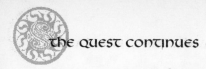

she said proudly, "this is Ross McBride – Marnie's father."

Becky's mouth hung open. She looked as horrified as Marnie felt.

The door to the boys' cabin burst open, sending Edwin into a flurry of fluttering hysterics. "Arrrrghhhh!" he squawked. "Don't hurt me! I'm just standing guard!"

"It's *me*," said Kyle. Then he looked stern. "But if it hadn't have been…" He drew an explanatory finger across his throat.

Edwin gulped. He watched silently as Kyle rummaged around under his mattress, eventually pulling out the ancient arrow. Then the boy knelt down and examined the wooden wall panels. One came loose with just a few tugs, opening just far enough for Kyle to slot the arrow behind before pulling it back into place.

Kyle's instructions were brief and to the point. "Defend the Arrow of Truth with your life." The door banged shut behind him.

Edwin flapped awkwardly down to the floor and then sidled over to the arrow's hiding place, ready to begin his watch.

Deep in the misty wood, Nathaniel sat cross-legged by his campfire, studying the peculiar rock in his hands. The grey rock looked as if it had been chiselled and painted to show a rusty-red bear – but, of course, it hadn't. This was the rock that held Bruno prisoner.

Closing his eyes, Nathaniel drew his hand across the rock. It glimmered and shook for a moment. Then, Bruno leapt from its surface. "Thank you, Mr Stone, sir," he said politely.

"You're very welcome," replied the Native American.

But despite his release, Bruno didn't look happy.

"If you've got something to say," said Nathaniel, "just say it."

Bruno shuffled to and fro. "I'm very grateful that you've rescued me, sir," he said. "It wasn't any fun being stuck in that rock with the water level rising, I can tell you."

Nathaniel smiled encouragingly. "What's on your mind?" he said.

"Well, you see," said Bruno hesitantly, "I was... I was waiting for Marnie. It's just that... well... she put me in that rock... and, er... well..." He took a deep breath as if summoning all his courage. His next words were confidently spoken. "I want you to put me back in the rock, sir. Marnie needs the chance to do the right thing."

"And what if she does the wrong thing?" asked Nathaniel.

"Then I'm no worse off," said Bruno seriously. "I'm already a stone bear."

Nathaniel chuckled to himself, then nodded his head towards Bruno. "It's not every day an old *wichasha wakan* gets to bow to the wisdom of a little stone bear," he said.

Mr McBride tilted the plastic hoop this way and that, carefully examining the spider's web of twine that was stretched across it. He twanged a couple of threads. "What did I tell you?" he said wryly. "Camp's so important for developing these crucial life skills."

"What are you doing?" asked Marnie.

"I'm trying to catch dreams, I think."

This wasn't what Marnie had meant at all. "What are you doing with *her*?" she repeated.

There was an uncomfortable pause, while the noisy chatter of reunited parents and children taking part in the activity session ebbed and flowed around them.

"I know it's a bit of a shock," said Mr McBride eventually. "But she seems like a wonderful person. Can't you just give her a chance?"

"She's *not* a wonderful person!" snapped Marnie. "She's just *using* you." At once, she realised that she'd hurt him deeply.

"Oh, I see. She's using me for my powerful connections in the land of TV," Mr McBride said slowly. "She's after my fabulous riches."

There was only one option now. It wasn't fair and it wasn't right, but Marnie knew that it was her only chance to outwit Aurora... and Toledo. "You don't understand," began Marnie. Then she went for the jugular. "She's not Mom."

Mr McBride regarded at her sadly, then stretched an arm round her sagging shoulders. "She'll never replace your mother, sweetheart," he said. "But Mom wanted both of us to be get on with our lives. She didn't want us to be lonely."

Marnie's heart, which had leapt with her father's first words, now dropped like a stone. She made one last attempt. "But we've got each other. We don't *need* anyone else."

"But wouldn't it be good for you to have a woman to talk to?" said her dad hopefully.

Marnie didn't have to take this. She stood up, her chair scraping back across the floor. "I talk to *Mom*," she said, and left the room.

Becky was having an equally tough time. "He's really not your type," she insisted, trying to keep up with Aurora as she stalked around the camp. "He's nice, he's polite, and he seems, well, *normal*."

Her mother's eyes darkened. "I'm not looking for love lessons from an eleven-year-old girl," she snarled. "Now, where's that torn page I asked you to find?"

"Is that all you care about?" Becky took a step back.

Aurora changed tack. "Darling," she said serenely. "I'm under a lot of pressure with the new show. But if you don't want to help me—"

"I looked, but I couldn't find it, OK?" snapped Becky. Carefully avoiding her mother's intense gaze, she spotted a beige-clad figure coming their way. "Here's your new boyfriend," she said. "Maybe *he* knows where it is."

As Aurora swung round to face Ross McBride, a dazzling smile transformed her face. She patted Becky's hand clumsily. "Run along and join your friends, dear. We'll see you at the archery competition."

Becky went. And she didn't have to go far before she bumped into someone just as fed up as she was herself.

Marnie was slumped on the steps leading to the main cabin, her chin cupped in her hands. "OK," she said to Becky. "This is gross."

"And weird," agreed Becky. "My mom's acting like a teenager."

"My dad tried to give me the won't-it-be-nice-to-have-another-woman-to-talk-to speech," said Marnie grimly.

"Good luck," said Becky. "*I* can't even talk to her. I used to. But now, it's like she's not even there."

Better than anyone, Marnie recognised that feeling.

"Your mom!" gasped Becky, her cheeks burning with colour. "I forgot – I'm so sorry!"

But Marnie wasn't offended. If anything, she was starting to realise that she and Becky might not be so different after all. "That's OK," she said. "But I do know what you mean about not having a mother to talk to any more."

Becky stared into space, as if remembering the old

174

Aurora. "For eleven years," she said wistfully, "it's just been me and Mom. And now I'm supposed to cheer because she's got a boyfriend?"

"We'll see about that…" said Marnie. She was determined that her dad and Aurora wouldn't become an item. But first, she had to get that arrow… Quickly making her excuses, she went directly to Kyle's cabin. Instinct told her that this was where the arrow would be. And, when she found Edwin standing guiltily by a loose wall panel, common sense told her that she'd found it.

The Arrow of Truth was hers.

CHAPTER TWENTY

The ARROW
Of TRUTH

"Let the Arrow of Truth and the Bow of Wisdom guide your every shot," Gramps announced to crowd gathered around the archery field. "Let the games begin!"

Marnie looked round at the eager parents, who clapped enthusiastically, then jostled for a better view of the target. With a sinking heart, she saw that Aurora stood next to Mr McBride, hanging on to his arm and, it seemed, his every word.

Thuck! Becky's arrow hit one of the outer rings of the target. There was a smattering of applause and Becky walked despondently back to her clan.

Now it was Marnie's turn. Confidently, she plucked an arrow from the holder and strode forwards. She had the Arrow of Truth in her possession – she could *win* this. Readying her arrow, she took aim, focussing all her power at the dead centre of the target and pulling back her bow, when—

"Why all this conflict and strife when we both want the same thing?" whispered Toledo's voice. "And now that we're practically family…"

Marnie's arm began to tremble, then shook so badly that she could no longer aim at the target. But she gripped the bow more tightly, using her own dark power to battle for supremacy against Aurora and her evil host. She steadied her arm and fired.

"Bullseye!" shouted Mr McBride. "Good shot, Marnie!"

For a few wonderful seconds, Marnie basked in the glow of her perfect score… until Kyle fired his shot. Another bullseye. Unexpected anger coursed through her, robbing her of all reason and leaving behind a furious desire to get even.

Marnie looked at her watch – there was just enough time… She slipped away from the archery field and hurried through the trees towards the main cabin.

The cool, dark atmosphere inside had no effect on Marnie's hunger for revenge. She marched towards an antique wooden dresser, then systematically wrenched open its tiny drawers. Only one drawer refused to open – and that stood no chance against the powers of evil. Marnie concentrated all her energy on the lock, and smiled as it clicked open. Inside was an ornate golden key, which she pocketed at once. Next, she turned her attention to the glass display case that hung on the wall above, firing another burst of energy at the Bow of Wisdom displayed there. *Pouf!* It vanished. Now, all that she had to do was hide the key.

Marnie reached the archery field just in time to hear her grandpa announce the results.

"We're down to our final two competitors," he said proudly. "Marnie and Kyle!"

While Mr McBride clapped loudly, Aurora fixed Marnie with her ebony eyes. "It feels good to have power again, doesn't it?" whispered Toledo. Aurora smiled.

Marnie lifted her bow, aimed, fired. The crowd roared its approval as her arrow pierced the centre of the target once more.

Now, it was Kyle's turn. He calmly let his arrow fly and it shot through the air, heading straight towards the bullseye. Then, just as it was about to hit home, the arrow inexplicably slowed and hung motionless before the target. It dropped harmlessly onto the grass.

Marnie gave a satisfied smile.

"Congratulations!" shouted Gramps. "You're the winner!"

"Bravo, Marnie," whispered Toledo. "I can help you have it all – anything your little heart desires…"

Marnie turned triumphantly to her team, noting with some surprise that nobody seemed terribly enthusiastic and, in fact, appeared to be far more interested in fiddling with buttons and hairclips than congratulating her. She shrugged it off.

But Marnie's win wasn't the only event to inspire bad feeling that day. When everyone returned to the main cabin, Gramps made a dreadful discovery. "If this was meant as a prank," he said seriously, "then it wasn't funny. The Bow of Wisdom has gone. And unless the person responsible steps forward, every bag will be searched."

There was silence.

To everyone's surprise, Marnie took a tentative step forward. "I don't want to accuse anyone," she said in a small voice, "but I... I saw Kyle take that key."

"What?" cried Kyle. "I didn't!" he protested. Then, when no one spoke, he added desperately, "She's lying!"

The old Marnie would have confessed immediately. But the old Marnie was hidden beneath so many layers of evil that she couldn't be heard. Instead, she simply joined the silent throng that followed Gramps and Kyle to the luggage pile.

"OK, which one is yours?" asked Gramps. Everyone watched as he rifled through Kyle's belongings. And, within seconds, he had pulled a golden key from inside a zippered compartment. Gramps looked saddened and disappointed.

Kyle said nothing at all. He simply hung his head and waited for his punishment.

Strangely, Kyle's self-control affected Marnie far more than any outburst would have done. Never had she felt so ashamed of herself. Silently, she retrieved her backpack and took it into the woods where, safe from onlookers, she freed Edwin, Ailsa and Hunter. They looked at her disapprovingly.

"Can't you sssee what'sss happening?" hissed Ailsa. "It'sss the Book! It'sss poisssoning you, just like it poisssoned Michael."

Marnie gasped in horror. She *did* see, with awful clarity, what the Book had done to her… Overnight, it had changed her into a person so evil, so truly vile, that she was prepared to accept Toledo's promises in exchange for that magnificent, yet terrible prize she sought – *The Book of Forbidden Knowledge* itself.

Now that Michael was gone, there was only one person who could help Marnie. And, summoning all of her strength, she closed her eyes and tried to connect. The effort left her weak and trembling, but when her eyelids fluttered open again, she saw that she'd done it. She was in the middle of the familiar, misty wood and there, sitting beside a small campfire, was Nathaniel. He looked shocked and anxious.

"You've got to be real careful with that magic power stuff," he warned. "You don't want to end up someplace that you didn't mean to go."

Marnie took a deep breath – and then the words came tumbling out. "I… I don't know what's happening to me," she said. "One minute, I'm fine, the next minute, I say something really mean to someone or… or I do something horrible. It's like I… I… I

180

can't help it. It's almost like I've turned into… into *Evil Marnie*—"

"Sit," said Nathaniel. "Breathe. Stop talking." He handed her a bunch of fresh sage. "Take this and breathe in, breathe out."

But the calming herbs did little to relax Marnie. "Can you cure me?" she asked urgently. "I just want to be like *myself* again."

"This is bad stuff you're involved in," said Nathaniel quietly, his eyes cast down. "It's not going to be easy."

Aurora Dexter was rapidly losing control. She attacked the heap of luggage, ripping open each bag and spilling out its contents, before moving on to the next. But she still hadn't found what she was looking for.

Becky watched nervously. Then, as if she could stand the destruction no longer, she whispered, "It's that one."

"Huh?" Aurora glared at her daughter briefly, then directed her attention to Marnie's blue backpack, which she set upon with the ferocity of a wild beast. At first, the bag yielded nothing but black clothes, but then Aurora dug deep, pulling out the framed photo of Marnie's mother.

"Mom!" hissed Becky.

Aurora ignored her. She turned over the frame and flipped open the backing to reveal a thick square of paper. "Finally…" she breathed. With trembling fingers, she opened up the page, before hurriedly folding it once more and stumbling to her feet. "Camp's over," she said, her husky voice a mixture of urgency and excitement. "Let's go, sweetie!" She walked away, carelessly treading on Marnie's photo frame as she went. The glass shattered beneath her white shoe.

Hastily, Becky stuffed Marnie's belongings into her backpack, before hurrying after her mother and running – *oof!* – into Mr McBride instead.

"Whoa there!" he said. "Are you all right?"

As Becky nodded nervously, Mr McBride spotted her mother moving swiftly away. "Aurora!" he called. "I just wanted to apologise about Marnie's behaviour and… and I wondered if perhaps—"

Aurora cut him off. "It's OK, Ross," she said briskly. "I understand. It's not the right time." She turned to go.

"No, wait!" he called.

Aurora looked back one last time, her eyes cold and unfeeling. "Goodbye, Ross," she said firmly, before taking Becky's hand and dragging her away.

Mr McBride stared after them both for a moment. "Well, I'll see you around, I guess…" he said.

Nathaniel remained silent for what seemed like hours, but Marnie knew to be just minutes. Then slowly, carefully, he reached out and smoothed his fingers over her forehead.

Zzz… Marnie felt a fizz of power leap from her to the Native American. He jerked his hand away, and stared at Marnie in horror. His fingers shook spasmodically, as if he'd received an electric shock.

"Clear your mind," he said urgently. "Think about *nothing*. You have to relax or I can't help you."

And Marnie tried to relax. She closed her eyes tightly and really tried. But she could still feel the dark power that had overtaken her, fighting off any attempt to banish it.

Pzzzzzt! She clutched her head in agony as a huge power surge ricocheted around her body and then through her mind. And when she opened her eyes, both Nathaniel and the wood had vanished.

Stunned and confused, she staggered through the camp, looking for something she recognised – something to reassure her that she hadn't gone totally crazy. With relief, she spotted her backpack and crouched beside it. Then her heart sank. There, wrapped in a black scarf, was her precious photo, the glass shattered, but her mother's loving expression intact. With fingers that trembled so badly she could hardly hold it, Marnie turned over the photo frame.

The torn page, of course, was gone.

CHAPTER TWENTY-ONE

The Magic
is Awakened

The car juddered to a halt, shaking Marnie to wakefulness and rescuing her from yet another nightmare – this time, reliving Wolfgang's horrific death by fire. She opened her eyes and saw her grandparents' country home.

"Marnie? We're here," said Dad gently. "Are you OK?"

"I'm just tired, I guess," she muttered.

But her father wasn't satisfied. "You don't seem yourself," he said. "Being rude to adults, falling out with your friends. You've changed, Marnie."

"*I've* changed?" spluttered Marnie. "What about *you*? I suppose you think that showing up to camp with Becky's mom is *totally* normal?"

"Sweetheart, we talked about that," said her dad. "Look, I know that sometimes I don't understand you, but I think even your mother would worry about

184

you now."

Marnie turned on him. "But she's not here, is she?" she stormed.

A range of emotions chased across Mr McBride's face – sadness, hurt and finally despair. "I miss her too," he said softly. "If I could bring her back, I would… But she's gone."

Marnie felt her heart harden. If her dad was too weak to do anything about it, then that was his problem. She was the Chosen One, she had the power to bring Mom back and *she would do it*.

Grandma bent down by Mr McBride's window. "Hey, how's my little girl?" she said cheerily.

Why did everyone keep treating her like a child? Unable to stomach their feeble comments a moment longer, Marnie snatched up her backpack and clambered out of the car. As she strode away into the wood, Dad shouted ineffectually after her. "Don't you dare walk away from me, young lady!"

Just watch me, thought Marnie.

Aurora Dexter sank back into her white leather armchair and gazed greedily at the old, crinkled piece of paper in her hands. The ancient runes glowed with an ethereal light, then shimmered and danced, before returning to their original positions. But there was something new.

"The wolf rune," said Aurora softly. "An eagle, a bear, a snake and now a wolf. My little Wolfie, what a

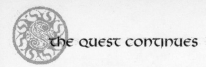

strange twist of fate that *you* should be the one to lead her to the Book…" She laughed maniacally as she rose from her chair and approached the shining mask. "Give me the eyes," she breathed.

Marnie stomped along the deserted trail, deeper and deeper into the ever-darkening wood. Eventually, frustrated and exhausted, she came to a halt and pulled Edwin and Ailsa from her backpack.

"Look," she said sternly, a threatening frown distorting her features. "If you ever want to be human again, you'd better start helping me."

The two creatures cowered fearfully before her.

"*Ow-owww!*" The eerie cry of a wolf echoed in the distance, distracting Marnie from her interrogation. And, even though Aurora had stolen her clues, the truth was revealed at last.

"Wolfgang," Marnie whispered. "A snake rune, a bear rune, an eagle run… The wolf rune has got to be next, right?" New hope surged through her. "That's the puzzle," she continued, her voice rising to a crescendo. "That's what the torn page has been trying to tell me all along. I've got to bring Wolfgang back!"

Edwin and Ailsa glanced at each other in dismay, but nothing they could say or do would stop Marnie now. Nothing.

She raised her hands skywards and took a deep, shuddering breath. Then, channelling all the dark power within her, she visualised Wolfgang... his blue and gold coat, his beautifully carved fur, his proud eyes...

"Come to me, Wolfgang!" she cried. "Come to me, I command you! For *I am your master!*"

A ghostly image began to materialise in mid-air. It was Wolfgang's face, wreathed in flames. Writhing in torment, the little wolf opened his eyes and looked imploringly at Marnie. "Why do you torment me?" he moaned. "Why can you not leave me in peace...?"

His pitiful plea did little to penetrate Marnie's icy soul. "Do you know the secrets of the spirit world?" she demanded. When Wolfgang nodded reluctantly, she pressed him further. "Then, will you lead me to the Book?"

"I can *not!*" said Wolfgang.

"Can not or *will* not?" said Marnie coldly.

"You have been corrupted," was Wolfgang's reply. "The power of the Book is too strong..."

Marnie narrowed her eyes, concentrating her power on the little wolf. Immediately, the flames encircling him leapt and danced with renewed vigour, and Wolfgang yelped in pain.

"All right," the wolf moaned. "I'll take you as far as my spirit allows, but stop tormenting me, *please!*" His face slowly faded away, until all that remained was a ghostly howl that echoed throughout the woods.

Like a sleepwalker, Marnie followed the melancholy sound.

In another wood, where mist wove in and out of the trees, a little wooden horse danced impatiently around a small campfire.

"I'm a nag of action," grumbled Hunter. "It isn't my style, sitting here on my rump, twiddling my fetlocks!"

From Kyle's troubled expression, it looked as if he thought the same way. "We can't just sit here when Marnie's in trouble," he said to his grandpa.

"You've got to let her walk her path," Nathaniel replied solemnly, although his words carried little conviction. He looked tired and frail, as if he'd aged overnight. "That's our way, grandson."

Kyle grew increasingly agitated. "But something's really wrong!" he insisted. "Lying, stealing, cheating… What is she going to do *next*?"

Hunter bounced onto Nathaniel's knee. "Why did she want that old bow and arrow anyway?" he asked.

The old Native American bent his head and stared into the flames of the campfire. "She has a deep purpose in mind," he said gravely. "She'll destroy them or use them…"

"So what?" said Kyle, springing to his feet. "Are we just going to wait and see if she does good or bad?"

The cry of a wolf sounded in the distance, and Nathaniel looked up. "You're right, grandson," he said. "The darkness has spread. There's only one thing left to do."

McTaggart was still trapped inside a weasel's body, inside a glass prison, inside Toledo the Shapeshifter's dazzling white room. It was playing havoc with his nerves.

"All is lost!" he cried, flinging himself against the glass for the eleven hundredth time. "I'm not a wizard! I have no power! How's a wee weasel supposed to help the Chosen One?"

The answer came from a totally unexpected source.

Slowly a figure began to take shape in Room 1111. It became more and more distinct until McTaggart took notice at last, staring in amazement at his old master.

"Trust yourself, man," said Michael Scot. "You have more power than you know. *Believe* in yourself and you may yet win the day."

The ghostly image faded.

"I've got to get out of here!" muttered McTaggart, more urgently now.

But help was nearer at hand than he ever could have guessed. Edwin and Ailsa, who had hung back as Marnie headed off in the direction of the howling wolf, had decided that it was time they furthered the Quest.

"Why did I ever let you talk me into thisss?" hissed Ailsa, as they flew over hills and valleys. She wrapped herself more tightly around Edwin and clung on for dear life.

With a near-expert flick of his metal wings, Edwin

changed direction and soared towards the Fairmont Springs Hotel. "We need to help Marnie," he said. "We need to draw the evil out of her. We need some *magic!*"

"Yesss!" agreed Ailsa, as they skimmed the treetops. "But why are we going to Michael'sss palace when Michael isss long gone?"

"Michael may be long gone," said Edwin, puffing a little with the exertion of flying and speaking at the same time, "but his power may not be." And, much to Ailsa's horror, he dived towards the ornate building below, rocketing straight through a top window.

Awestruck, McTaggart watched as they bounced across the marble floor, then slid to halt in an undignified heap.

Edwin leapt to his feet and shook himself before proudly proclaiming, "The eagle has—"

"Crasssh landed," said Ailsa, uncoiling herself gingerly. "Ssso, now we're here, what exxxactly isss your plan?"

"Sssimplicity itssself," mimicked Edwin. "We turn McTaggart back into, well, McTaggart. Then he pretends to be Michael – with his cloak and staff – and he persuades Marnie to do the right thing." He puffed out his chest proudly. "Well?"

"And how exactly do you propose to do that?" squeaked an insistent voice from the tabletop.

For the first time, Edwin looked up at the furry creature he'd earmarked for a starring role in his plan. He gulped. "Oh, surely we can do a simple thing like turn a weasel back into McTaggart?" he said uncertainly.

"If Michael were here, he'd do it with a wave of hisss wizard'sss ssstaff," said Ailsa, tilting her golden head regally to acknowledge the brilliance of her idea.

"Then let's try it!" announced Edwin.

The little eagle hopped and fluttered towards Michael's staff, which leaned a nearby wall, and curved his wings around the bottom. Ailsa joined him, coiling her body around the dark wood. Together, they heaved with all their might. But it didn't budge.

"We'll never ssshift it," groaned Ailsa. "It'sss againssst the lawsss of physsssicssss!"

"We are working with the laws of *magic*, you sssilly ssserpent!" insisted Edwin. "See? It *is* moving."

And it was true. Miraculously, marvellously, magically, Michael Scot's staff swung upright until it was balanced precariously. Then it toppled, falling unstoppably towards the glass case until... *Crash!* The great wizard's staff made contact with McTaggart's prison, sending a great burst of energy fizzing and crackling all around. There was a blinding flash of light and, when the smoke cleared, a life-size and totally human McTaggart stood on the table. Dressed in his familiar tartan, Michael Scot's dark cloak hung from his shoulders and in his hand was the magic staff. He wore the now-useless glass cage like a crown.

"Behold!" cried Edwin. "The great Michael Scot!"

CHAPTER TWENTY-TWO

The Falls of Faith

Marnie strode onwards, slowing only to deal with the obstacles that nature had strewn in her path. Gnarly tree roots, low branches and vast, prickly bushes – she left them all far behind her in her search for the Book. And always, in the distance, there was the mournful sound of a howling wolf.

"In your heart, you know this is wrong…" echoed Wolfgang's voice.

"What's wrong?" Marnie gasped, as she leapt up a small bank.

The reply was swift. "What you are planning to do?"

"You don't *know* what I'm going to do," said Marnie.

Wolfgang's face appeared before her, ringed by flame. "You want your mother back," he said. "That's natural. But trying to do it… that's wrong."

In a small, secret part of her soul that was untouched

by the Book's dark power, Marnie knew he was right. But she couldn't stop now. She was too close – and her mother was too near. "Just shut up and keep going!" she snapped guiltily. "You *swore* to help me!"

So the Quest continued. And not just for Marnie. Following in her footsteps was a woman in a white suit.

Nathaniel, Kyle and Hunter stared at the old, blackened woodshed, leaping back as its doors burst open to reveal the rattling, pulsating monster within. Like evil eyes, the generator's yellow dials glared balefully at them. Wraithlike tentacles sprang, glittering, from the machine, reaching out towards the intruders.

"It's too dangerous!" shouted Nathaniel above the racket. "You must go now!"

Hunter didn't need telling twice. He was off, like a bullet from a gun.

Kyle hesitated. "I'm not going anywhere without you, Grandpa," he said.

"I've got to stay and look after the Book," mumbled Nathaniel, fumbling with the generator's controls. The effort left him visibly shaken, and his words were slurred. But his grandson grasped their meaning.

"The Book?" Kyle said slowly.

"Yes – may the spirits forgive me – the Book!" cried Nathaniel. "Now, go!"

Kyle didn't move. "All this time, you knew it was here?"

Nathaniel ignored his question, as his fingers darted about the machine, shutting off valves, adjusting pistons, flicking switches – all to no effect. "Back to the campfire," he commanded. "You'll be safe there. *Go!*"

Reluctantly, Kyle went.

At long last, Marnie emerged from the wood to find herself on a rocky outcrop above a huge waterfall. The air was filled with sound and spray.

Wolfgang's ghostly face appeared again. "I'll go thus far and no further," he said firmly.

"You mean, this is *it*?" said Marnie. "This is where the Book is?" She looked doubtfully across the smooth rock to the waterfall beyond. There were no golden caskets, no deep crevices... There was nowhere to hide *The Book of Forbidden Knowledge*. Had she been tricked?

"On the other side, you may find what you are looking for..." Wolfgang's voice had begun to quaver, and his image became paler.

"Wait!" Marnie said desperately.

"Goodbye, child," Wolfgang whispered. "You are still the Chosen One. The choice to do right or do wrong is still yours..." He faded away, until all that remained was a tiny lick of flame. The flame went out.

"Stop, I command you!" cried Marnie.

Chief Stone Bear reached the waterfall, then he flung the Book into the air... It plunged over the edge of the cliff towards the waterfall, vanishing instantly... Stone Bear stepped off the edge of the rock, but instead of tumbling into the water, a stone path began to materialise beneath his feet... After taking a couple of steps, the Native American disappeared too...

As the images whirled around Marnie's mind, she suddenly realised what she must do to claim the Book. She had to take the terrifying leap of faith and walk above the cascading waterfall.

Toledo's persuasive whisper entered her thoughts. "There is a path, little one. It's so easy... Just a few steps and the Quest will be over."

Hands dug deep into soil, shovelling it away to create a deep hole... Chief Stone Bear carefully wrapped the gleaming Book in a hides... He dropped the bundle into the hole and placed a bunch of sage at each corner...

Indecision raged within Marnie. She took a step forward, nearer to the edge of the cliff. Beneath her feet, a rocky path began to appear, forming a bridge across the waterfall. It stretched to the other side where Wolfgang had told her she would find what she was looking for.

"It's so easy," said Aurora, walking from the trees where she'd remained hidden. "Just a few steps.... Cross through the illusion with me. Find the Book and, with it, your mother, who loves you so dearly." She smiled encouragingly. "Come, we are so close."

Horrified, Marnie looked back. So, despite all her efforts to keep Toledo and his human servant at bay, the Shapeshifter was here with her at the end, tempting her with irresistible thoughts of her mother. Could she do it? Dare she?

But before she had the chance to decide, there was a flurry of swirling velvet, and a cloaked figure appeared out of nowhere. He was brandishing a staff, and for one brief, magical moment, Marnie thought it was Michael.

"No, mistress!" cried McTaggart.

"Oh, dear," said Aurora, looking him up and down. "If only the clothes *did* maketh the man."

McTaggart turned to face his enemy, his gaze stern and unflinching. "I may be no wizard," he said, "but I am the Keeper of the Book. And you shall not cross."

As if triggered by some unseen signal, Aurora and McTaggart ceased their argument, directing their appeals at Marnie instead.

"You are the Chosen One. The Book is *yours*, to do with as you wish…"

"No! You must use the Book to do good!"

"She misses you, Marnie. Don't you want to see her?"

"Don't listen! You don't know what you're doing!"

Like a knotted rope in a tug-of-war, Marnie edged first one way and then the other. But finally, her decision was made. Her eyes brimming with tears, she cast an apologetic look at McTaggart, then turned to face the waterfall. The rock bridge began to grow at her feet, creating a path to a magical world.

She stepped from the cliff onto the bridge – and vanished.

Nathaniel's fury was incredible to behold. Wielding a deadly axe, he rained a shower of blows on the generator, hacking mercilessly at its evil core, thumping, pounding until the it gave one last shuddering – almost human – sigh and the yellow lights flickered and died.

The old Native American dragged the lifeless machine aside to show a large, flat stone. This too, he pulled out of the way. Beneath, was cold, dark earth, which Nathaniel loosened with his fingernails, before plunging his hands into the soil. He dug quickly, deeper and deeper until the long-lost treasure that Chief Stone Bear had tried so hard to conceal was revealed in all its golden, glowing glory.... *The Book of Forbidden Knowledge.*

It took only a split-second for Nathaniel to realise that he was not alone.

Marnie McBride stared at him coldly. This was the man who had kept the Book, and its infinite power from her, the man who had kept *her own mother* from her.

"You must not do it!" said Nathaniel urgently.

But Marnie focussed all the hatred she felt into one bolt of dark energy and let it fly, watching as it crackled through the air like lightning.

Where Nathaniel had stood, there was now only a wisp of smoke.

High on the clifftop, Aurora faced McTaggart. "The Chosen One has made her choice," she said scornfully. "Don't you understand the second prophecy? You fool... Don't you know when I was born?"

McTaggart's answer was filled with dread. "The eleventh minute of the eleventh hour—"

"Of the eleventh day of the eleventh month!" Aurora finished impatiently. Her scarlet lips curved into a terrible smile. "The girl-child has led me to what is mine. And once I have the Book, I shall rise as... *the Dawn Queen*. Now, get out of my way!"

McTaggart wielded the staff, which began to glow with magic. "Man, woman or beast – by the power of Michael Scot, *begone*!" he cried.

Aurora pointed a finger, unleashing her anger with a flash that threw McTaggart to his knees. He stumbled to his feet and fought back strongly, directing the staff's power back at his enemy. But Aurora fixed him with a look of pure determination and attacked him with power so invincible that McTaggart was driven to the very brink of disaster. For a moment, he teetered on the edge of the cliff, then Michael Scot's trusty servant toppled and fell like a stone. The churning, boiling water at the foot of the waterfall swallowed him instantly.

Marnie McBride gazed in wonder at *The Book of Forbidden Knowledge*, unable to believe that she'd done it. She'd reached the end of the Quest. The Book was hers, at last!

She reached down, aching to touch the soft leather cover, to lift the Book from its cold, damp grave… But when she was just a hair's breadth away, long, manicured fingers sprouted from the ground. They curled around the precious Book and swiftly pulled it down, down, down into the waiting earth. It vanished from sight, taking Marnie's dreams with it.

"*No!*" she cried.

The generator let out a hideous scream and lurched back to life. The shed doors slammed shut. The lock slid into place, trapping Marnie inside. Spectacularly, the shed exploded in a ball of flame.

"Marnie!" cried Mr McBride.

She opened her eyes to find that she was not dead. Instead, she was back where she'd started, perched precariously on the edge of the cliff.

Dad approached her cautiously. "Step away from there," he said gently. "Come on, *please.*"

Marnie could do no more than stare, first at Dad, then down at the churning water at the bottom of the waterfall.

"Oh, what a dance we have danced," echoed Toledo's gleeful voice. "And, in the end, it was you, girl-child, who led me straight to what is mine. *My* Book, dear Marnie… *Mine.*"

Angry tears spilled down Marnie's cheeks. She had tried so hard to get her mother back, and all for

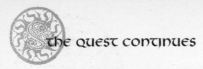

nothing. Urgently, she wracked her brains. If she had help… could she try again? Was there still a chance? She whirled round to face her father. "You said that you would do *anything* to bring Mom back!" she cried desperately. "Did you *mean* it?"

For seconds, Dad said nothing. Then he took a deep breath. "No, sweetheart. I didn't mean it," he said softly. "Mom's gone. She can't come back, no matter how much we want her to." He paused, and his eyes welled with tears. "But she's in our hearts. For ever."

And Marnie knew that he was right. She began to cry – big, painful sobs that shook her body and released the pain that she had held inside for so long. She ran to her father, burying herself deep in his welcoming arms. She wept and wept, hardly aware that as she did so, the dark power that had held her captive was seeping away, along with her grief.

CHAPTER TWENTY-THREE

The Calm
Before the Storm

Marnie sat bolt upright in bed, the terrifying nightmare still crystal clear. Again and again, the Dawn Queen had reached for the Book, and nothing Marnie did could stop her. She rubbed her eyes, as if that would erase the image from her troubled mind, and looked up. At the foot of her bed stood a ghostly hooded figure.

"Michael?" she whispered.

"I am just a spirit, child," murmured the great wizard, pushing back the hood. His craggy face shimmered in and out of focus, like a television picture during a storm.

Marnie took a deep breath, not knowing quite how to approach the subject. "McTaggart..." she began.

"He was honest and true, both wiser and more steadfast than his master," said Michael. "He showed courage right to the end in trying to save you... and

201

in trying to save the Book."

"But *she* has the Book," said Marnie. "I failed. The Quest is over."

Michael shook his head. "The power of the Book corrupted you, but you passed that test. The darkness is gone from you now and the power of goodness shines through – a power you must use wisely." His gaze was unflinching. "I was a fool to write the Book, but the world should not suffer for my greed and stupidity."

All at once, Marnie knew what she must do. "I have to destroy the Book," she breathed.

"To succeed, your power must be joined by that of another Chosen One," said Michael. "The power of the Shoebox Zoo must be reunited. Two of them are missing – find them, just as you found yourself." His image started to fade.

"Wait!" There was something Marnie needed to ask. "If you see my mother, tell her that I love her and I miss her," she said. She smiled. "But tell her that I'm OK."

The great wizard was gone. But his reply floated through Marnie's mind. "She already knows, child…"

The old Marnie was back. Her energy no longer sapped by the Book, she felt brighter, happier and so positive that *nothing* seemed beyond her reach. Defeating the Dawn Queen and destroying the Book – easy. Making it up with Kyle – a little harder.

Cautiously, she approached the space under the trees where the generator shed had once been. Kyle sat on a lump of wood, in the middle of the scarred landscape, smoking debris scattered all around him. He stared forlornly into the distance.

"I didn't know the Book was going to be here," said Marnie timidly. She squatted down beside Kyle. "But the Quest isn't over – Michael just told me so."

Kyle wouldn't look at her. "I don't care about your stupid book or your stupid wizard," he muttered. "I just want to know where my grandfather is."

With a shiver, Marnie remembered what she'd done – how she'd turned her powers on Nathaniel when all he'd wanted to do was protect her. It didn't matter that she'd been corrupted by the evil power of the Book. She'd done it. And now she'd have to undo it. "I don't know where he is," she said quietly. "But I'll help you—"

Kyle turned on her, his eyes blazing with anger. They were red-rimmed too, as if he'd been crying for a long time. "I don't want your kind of help, not after what you did to Bruno!" he shouted. "Just leave me alone." He stalked away, a wooden dance stick of a horse held tightly in his hand.

It was time for Marnie to make amends. She made her way to the river's edge, where she wouldn't be disturbed. With eyes tight shut, she focussed her thoughts on Bruno, drawing him closer, willing him to appear. She peeped nervously, turning weak with relief when she realised that it had worked. There before her was the rock in which she'd imprisoned dear, trusty Bruno. Marnie drew her hand across the stone – and the little stone bear was free! He yawned and stretched with delight.

"I'm *so* sorry," said Marnie.

"It's not your fault – it's the Book's fault," Bruno said firmly. "The evil power of the Book tempted you, poisoning your mind with dark thoughts. It corrupted you, just like it's always done. It tempted the great Michael Scot too – and other people, with stronger wills than his, through the ages." He chuckled. "I'm amazed a wee lassie like yourself resisted it so long!"

As Marnie listened to his kind, understanding words, she braced herself to share the bad news.

Bruno seemed to realise that something was wrong. "What's the matter?" he said gently.

"It's McTaggart," whispered Marnie. "He's gone."

"No!" Bruno gasped, his soft brown eyes widening in horror.

"And I can't do this alone…" added Marnie. It was true. She needed all the help she could get.

Suddenly, as if responding to her plea, there was a flash of light at the very edge of her vision. Marnie turned her head and saw the silver tip of Michael's magical staff. Unthinkingly, she grasped the staff and was pulled into the mystical wood where she'd met Nathaniel. But this time, she saw McTaggart – a faded, ghostly version of the faithful servant, but McTaggart nonetheless.

Fresh tears sprang into her eyes. "Why did you have to leave me too?" she said sadly.

"I'm sorry," said McTaggart, his image shimmering in the half-light. "I tried my best."

"But what am I going to do?" Marnie pleaded. "I can't defeat a prophecy!"

"Mistress, you have more strength than you know," said the ghostly spirit. "You are the Chosen One." He smiled encouragingly. "My master gave me one last task to perform – to help you resolve his Quest. You can only do your best, Marnie. But trust me – that *will* be good enough."

She nodded tearfully.

"I'll always be with you," said McTaggart, as he began to fade from sight. "Listen to your heart... Believe in your dreams."

At once, Marnie was flung into another vision...

Chief Stone Bear opened the Book of Knowledge and light blazed from its pages, illuminating his horrified face... The chief hurled the Book towards the waterfall... With grim determination, he placed an arrow in his bow, took aim and fired...

For a moment, Marnie was stunned into silence. Then a feeling of pure happiness rushed through her. She now knew how to destroy the Book!

Slowly, she became aware of the two objects that she now held – the Bow of Wisdom and the Arrow of Truth. The loyal servant had not only helped her to find the solution to the Quest – he'd given her the tools to finish the job too. Silently, she thanked McTaggart from the bottom of her heart.

Then, unbelievably, things got a whole lot better. For there, walking through the misty wood, was the person she never thought she'd see again. He smiled, sending a road map of creases shooting across his kindly face.

"Nathaniel, you're OK!" cried Marnie. "I'm so sorry. I wasn't myself—"

He raised a hand to silence her. "It had to be so," he said firmly.

Marnie realised that the subject was now closed and felt yet another weight lift from her overburdened shoulders. "I just had a vision of Stone Bear at the waterfall," she said tentatively.

Nathaniel nodded wisely as he led her towards a small campfire. Marnie crouched beside it, grateful for its glowing warmth. The old Native American sat opposite her on a tree stump.

"The Falls of Faith," he said, as if speaking to himself. "There's an ancient tradition of the Lakota Sioux called the Vision Quest – a way of making contact with the spirit world and finding out the truth…" He gazed into the distance. "I had a vision of the Chosen One – a girl-child who was wise, strong and beautiful, like her mother… A girl-child who came across the great ocean to find a Book…"

With Nathaniel's softly spoken words had come a feeling of great calm. Marnie smiled – at last, everything was becoming clear.

"My job," explained Nathaniel, "and the job of those medicine men before me, was to keep the Book hidden, so its power couldn't get out into the world." He took a deep breath. "We thought we knew what we were doing, but maybe we got it wrong."

"Maybe now we've got a chance to put it right," said Marnie hopefully. But something else was bothering her. "I just don't know what to do about Kyle."

Nathaniel put his finger to his lips and gestured towards the fire. Marnie had seen so many incredible, unbelievable sights over the last year that it seemed almost natural that Kyle's image should be projected onto the flickering flames. He was talking to Edwin, Ailsa and Hunter. Marnie leant closer to listen.

"The Book is seriously dangerous, right?" he was saying. "It was like Michael made a ticking time bomb. It should have been his problem, but now it's Marnie's, and the way I see it, it's our problem too." He frowned thoughtfully. "I know she's done some pretty bad things, but we have to help her. That's what Grandpa said."

The relief was indescribable. Marnie looked at Nathaniel with tears in her eyes and rose obediently when he beckoned. Together, they walked out of the misty wood, towards Kyle, who was not so far away after all.

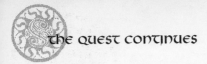

"Hey, look who I found!" she said.

Instantly, the sadness in Kyle's expression was replaced by pure joy. "Grandpa!" he shouted, leaping to his feet. He ran towards the old man and hugged him tightly.

But there was one more surprise to come.

"Boo!" said a small, gruff voice.

Edwin, Ailsa and Hunter dragged their eyes from the grandfather–grandson reunion and stared in jaw-dropping amazement at the little stone bear gambolling merrily in their direction.

"Bruno!" they shouted.

Marnie just beamed.

CHAPTER TWENTY-FOUR

ThE DAWN QUEEN RISES

Aurora Dexter was history. The quirky, eccentric star of *Above and Beyond*, whose blind ambition had led her to sign a pact with the devil, had gone. First, she had metamorphosed into the sophisticated, cruel, but oh-so-charming female vessel that held Toledo the Shapeshifter. Now that *The Book of Forbidden Knowledge* had been plucked from its hiding place, its terrible power had consumed her entirely, transforming her into a creature so loathsome, so utterly vile that only the merest trace of the original woman remained. The second prophecy had come true. She was the Dawn Queen.

Elegantly draped in a pure white cloak, she sat in front of the dressing-table mirror, admiring her reflection. Sleek, smooth auburn hair hung in perfectly straight curtains on either side of her deathly white face. Dark sunglasses completed the new look.

She smiled contentedly to herself, but that look changed to anger when the mirror misted over, clearing to show Toledo leering back at her.

The Dawn Queen snapped her fingers angrily and the reflection returned to normal. Then – *whoosh!* – Juan Roberto Montoya de Toledo was unceremoniously dragged from his host body, stretching like chewing gum, before landing with a thump on the marble floor.

"Now, that's more comfortable, isn't it?" drawled the Dawn Queen. Slowly, she turned to face him, removing her sunglasses to reveal chilling white eyes, pierced by jet-black pupils. They were fringed by thick, white eyelashes.

Toledo recoiled from her.

"What kind of a fool did you think I was?" she hissed. "You thought that you found me by chance, but it was I all along who was destined to become the Dawn Queen, and *I* who chose *you*."

Toledo laughed nastily. "You are simply Aurora Dexter, the poor cable TV clairvoyant from Valentine, Nebraska," he said.

The Dawn Queen spread the fingers of one hand and then clenched them tightly. But as she did so, it was Toledo who began to gasp for breath, as if she grasped not the air, but his long throat. "We had a contract," she hissed. "You wanted the Book. But I've got it *and I'm not giving it back*. My new network show demands *real* magic."

"Don't be fooled," croaked Toledo. "You have no real power without me."

"Wrong," replied the Dawn Queen. "I gave your body back to you, and now you work for me. Understand?"

Toledo nodded, stumbling back as she released him from her invisible grip. As if realising that resistance was futile, the Shapeshifter leaned casually against the dressing table, attempting to regain his composure – and the upper hand.

"We must open the Book on network television," he said. "The magic will seep into the minds of *millions* – a show with the highest ratings *ever*!"

"*I* must open the Book," she corrected him. Then, she paused, drumming her fingernails thoughtfully. "Hmm… The power spreads over the airwaves, through the ether, into those millions of living rooms, but we need those TVs to be switched *on* first."

Toledo nodded, as if eager to please.

"The seven deadly sins," mused the Dawn Queen.

"Pride, wrath, envy, lust…" Toledo paused hopefully, but his new mistress shook her head, so he continued. "Gluttony, sloth and—"

She turned to him, a demonic glint in her eye and, together, they chorused: "*Greed*!" They broke into peals of manic laughter, cut short by the sound of a door slamming. Hastily, the Dawn Queen slid on the sunglasses, to hide her bizarre eyes.

It was Becky. Hesitantly, she entered Room 1111,

as if unsure what she might find there. When she saw her mother − or rather, the monster that her mother had become − she drew back in horror. "Mom?" she said. "Is that you?"

"What do you want?" roared the Dawn Queen.

Becky's bottom lip began to tremble. "I live here, remember?" she whispered. She glanced at the tall, slender man in the white suit. "Is this your new boyfriend?" she said.

"Boyfriend?" Her mother snorted, as if the suggestion was thoroughly absurd. "Oh, dear me, no. Meet Juan Roberto Montoya de Toledo, the assistant for my show."

The look he directed back at the Dawn Queen was filled with fury.

Nathaniel smiled warmly at the gathered friends − Marnie, Kyle, Edwin, Ailsa and Hunter − together once more. Happily, they all smiled back. Marnie's smile was the widest of all.

The old Native American crouched down and placed a tattered bundle of hides on the ground. "Do you know what this is?" he asked.

"Why, it's your medicine bundle," said Hunter, as if the answer was obvious.

"That's right," said Nathaniel. "Every *wichasha wakan* has a medicine bundle − it's like a doctor's bag. And this is *my* medicine bundle. It goes right back to one of the greatest medicine men of them all − Chief

Stone Bear. My ancestor…"

Reverently, he began to unwrap the bundle, running his fingers over the strange and ancient objects held safely within – a necklace made of bear claws, a beaded eagle feather, a wolf's tail and the snake rattle that Marnie had found.

"The precious items you see here come from Stone Bear and three other great chiefs – Red Eagle, Two Wolves and Snake Tail," said Nathaniel.

The final pieces of the puzzle slotted into place. "Bear, snake, eagle, wolf," Marnie recited. "*The power of the Shoebox Zoo must now be reunited.* That's what Michael said."

Nathaniel looked up, his eyes brimming with sympathy and understanding. "Only there's one missing," he said.

"Wolfgang!" squawked Edwin.

Marnie nodded. She glanced at Kyle, who seemed stunned by the turn of events.

"I'm not going to tell you what to do," continued Nathaniel. "But it seems to me that it's no accident these creatures and the power of the four great medicine men match up."

Bruno politely raised a paw. "Excuse me, Mr Stone, sir," he said. "Why didn't you tell us this in the first place?"

Nathaniel looked a little shamefaced, but Marnie thought that she understood his reasons. "It wasn't his story to tell," she explained. "The Book was supposed to be found by the Chosen One – that's what this whole Quest has been about."

"Oh, that's all fine and dandy," said Edwin pompously. "But *that woman* has already got the Book."

The others looked on helplessly, and even Hunter seemed to sag.

"How can we stop her?" asked Bruno.

Marnie took a deep breath. There was no easy way of saying this, she knew. "We have to finish the Quest by destroying the Book," she told them.

There were neighs, squawks and howls of horror from ground level.

But Nathaniel remained calm. "I will help you where I can," he said.

"So will we," added Kyle. "Right guys?" He nodded at the small creatures clustered at his feet, who nodded vigorously.

Except Ailsa. She didn't say a word.

CHAPTER TWENTY-FIVE

COUNTDOWN
TO EVIL

"**S**ix... five... four... three..."
The floor manager signalled to the performers and crew that they were *On Air*, while a lone figure watched from the wings. Becky looked as if she was trying very hard not to cry.

The woman in white stared right into the camera lens. "Tune in to me, the Dawn Queen, tonight at eleven to eleven," she said imperiously. "Together, we will venture into perilous spirit realms, walk amongst shadows and share secrets of the unknown." She paused dramatically. "And I'll be telling you how you can win eleven million dollars – *tax free!*"

This was the programme that was on everybody's lips. Across the nation, excitement was growing, and speculation was rife. What was the show actually *about*? What did they have to *do* to win eleven million dollars? And, now that electricity had eventually been restored to the little painted house in the woods, even more viewers were hooked.

Except Grandma.

"Bobby, will you please dry the dishes?" she said, blocking the dazzling white glare from the TV set. "And turn this rubbish off!" She stomped back to the kitchen.

"What? When we just got the power back?" exclaimed Gramps. He turned to his son-in-law and rolled his eyes. "All right, dear. Whatever you say." He reached for the remote control as Marnie and Kyle burst into the room.

"No, wait!" said Marnie urgently. "Turn it up..." She stared at the screen, as the ultimate prize turned slowly on a revolving platform – *The Book of Forbidden Knowledge*. Her eyes alighted on Toledo, who stood beside the Book, managing to look both proud and envious at the same time.

"This magical, mystical volume," continued the Dawn Queen, "contains the answers to the questions closest to your heart. Why am I here? Is there an afterlife?" The camera zoomed in to show a close-up of her face – a stack of bank notes reflected in her designer sunglasses. "And will I win eleven million dollars?"

"Aurora did get her own show then," mused Mr McBride.

The Dawn Queen smiled alluringly. "Just tune in at eleven to eleven to watch as I open The Never-opened-in-eleven-hundred-years *Book of Forbidden Knowledge*! All you need to do is answer this simple question: How many elevens are in eleven hundred years…?"

Gramps chuckled delightedly. "Now, this sounds like a must-see show," he said.

But Marnie McBride's race against evil had lasted a long time, and she was determined not to fall at the final hurdle. "We've got to get to the TV studios," she whispered to Kyle.

In the safety of the attic room, Marnie unwrapped Nathaniel's medicine bundle to reveal the bear claw necklace, the silver snake rattle, the beaded eagle feather and the wolf's tail. Beside them, she reverently laid the Bow of Wisdom and the Arrow of Truth.

Ailsa reared up in all her hissing splendour. "*Sssssssssss!* You can't! You musssn't!"

"Are you sure about this, Marnie?" asked Kyle. He looked deeply uncertain.

She *was* sure – surer than she'd ever been about anything else in all her eleven years. "Trying to bring my mom back was wrong," she explained. "But look, bear, snake, eagle and wolf. That's what the clues have been trying to tell us all along."

"Ahem," said Hunter, clip-clopping in a circle. "And a horse too!"

Marnie stroked his prickly mane. "How could I forget Hunter?" she said. "A *horse*."

217

"But can you really do it?" asked Ailsa, her emerald eyes glinting.

"With a little help, I think I *can*," said Marnie thoughtfully, "because this time I'm doing it for *good*." It was true. Before, she'd been driven by the dark power of the Book. Now, she wanted to rid the world of its evil.

Everyone nodded. Sure now of their support, Marnie braced herself for the task that lay ahead. Balling her hands into fists, she shut her eyes tight and began to speak to the spirit world...

"Wolfgang?" she whispered. "Can you hear me?"

And, in the middle of a misty wood, an old Native American murmured his approval. "You may go home if you wish, little wolf," he said. "It's your choice."

There was an answering howl in the distance, which reached Marnie's ears too. "Wolfgang, we need your help," she pleaded. "Come on..."

The howling grew louder and louder, echoing all around the attic room until a beautifully carved wooden wolf materialised. Marnie softly stroked the blue and gold coat. "Wolfgang..." she whispered.

Incredulously, Kyle looked from Marnie to Wolfgang, then back to Marnie. "It worked," he said.

"You're *real*," chuckled Bruno, as he patted Wolfgang with his paw.

"Asss sssolid a lump of wood asss you ever were," agreed Ailsa, poking him with the tip of her tail.

At last, Wolfgang managed to find his voice. "I really

218

am alive?" he said, his voice croaky with disuse.

"You really *are*," said Marnie, laughing as the Shoe-box Zoo crowded together in a small, but perfectly formed group hug.

Hunter leapt onto the bed, glaring angrily at every-one. "Enough with all the happy families and pats on the back!" he neighed impatiently. "We've got *work* to do, remember?"

Wolfgang turned to him with a haughty gaze. "And who, precisely, are you?" he said.

Hunter snorted with irritation. "It doesn't matter who I am," he said. "It just matters that you're here, and now we can get on with it!"

"Get on with *what*?" enquired Wolfgang.

Marnie had watched the miniature pantomime for long enough. "Get on with destroying the Book," she told the little wolf. There wasn't time to explain. Quickly, she grabbed the ancient arrow and thrust the bow into Kyle's hand. "Now, concentrate," she said, closing her eyes, focussing her mind and summoning all of the power within her.

Immediately, an incredible roaring noise swirled around them. It was over in a second. But when Marnie cautiously opened her eyes, she saw not the wooden slats of the attic walls, but the smooth, white walls of a long corridor. This *had* to be the TV studios.

"Good heavens!" exclaimed Edwin, from some-where near her feet.

Kyle looked round in amazement. "Whew!" he whistled. "That was *cool*!"

"Come on!" said Marnie, looking nervously over her shoulder. "We'd better hide before someone sees us." She took flight, with Kyle close on her heels and Hunter in hot pursuit.

Bruno, Edwin and Wolfgang went to follow them, but Ailsa hissed warningly. "Not ssso fassst!" she said. "Do none of you realissse what'sss happening?"

The others stopped and looked back in surprise.

"We're sssigning our own death warrantsss," she cried. "Sssealing our own fate! Sssentencing oursssselves to life imprisssonment inssside thessse ridiculousss ssshellsss!" She pointed at each of them in turn. "A sssilly, ssslithering sssnake… A ssstupid ssstone bear… A moronic megal eagle…"

"What?" cried Edwin.

Ailsa ignored him. "And a woeful wooden wolf," she concluded. "Can't you sssee? That'sss what we'll remain for ever if the Book isss dessstroyed!"

Bruno stood his ground. "But if Aurora… er, Toledo… oh, whatever she is, is allowed to open the Book, then the whole world will be infected with its evil," he said, his honest face suffused with anxiety.

"I know," sighed Edwin. "But it would just be so good to be human again."

Ailsa flicked out her tongue and hissed her agreement. "*Ssso* good."

Not that far away, a painted wooden horse skidded to a halt and cocked his ears. As Marnie and Kyle ducked into a room, Hunter spun round on his hooves and, with a harrumph, galloped back the way he'd come, just in time to hear.

"We *must* play our part in destroying the Book," insisted Bruno, "even if we do remain like—"

"Like a bunch of selfish toy animals that's learnt nothing about nothing?" finished Hunter, rearing high above the Shoebox Zoo.

"What do *you* know?" squeaked Edwin, cowering beneath the flailing hooves.

"And who do you think you are?" asked Hunter, sticking his snout in Edwin's face. "Some wise wizard or something?"

Edwin mumbled an incoherent reply.

"Who knows why we're here?" continued Hunter. "Leave thinking about the meaning of life to folks who've got too much time on their hands." He paced to and fro. "I reckon we're put on this earth and we've got to do whatever we've got to do as best we can, no matter how tough the odds!"

"Oh, that's all we need!" cried Edwin. "*More* home-spun wisdom!"

"OK." Hunter leapt onto a nearby chair, continuing his stirring speech from on high. "If the Dawn Queen opens this Book of yours on TV, all that's bad is going to go right into good folks' living rooms all across the country, maybe all across the world."

The Shoebox Zoo gasped as one.

"We've got a chance to make things right." He paused, looking around the goggle-eyed group of silent animals. "A strong, noble eagle..."

Edwin blinked and then puffed out his chest proudly.

"...a big, beautiful bear, full of deep courage and wisdom..."

Bruno shyly shuffled his feet.

"...a snake that... that..." Hunter stopped, as if searching for the right word. "...that could spit poison in your eye!" he finished with a flourish.

Ailsa, who had been smiling in anticipation, frowned suspiciously, as if unsure whether this was a compliment or not.

"...a wolf who's passed through fire and death and I-don't-know-what-else..."

Wolfgang's gaze was steadfast and determined.

"...and a horse... OK, I'm just a horse," said Hunter modestly. "But this horse is going to put his life on the line! Those kids need our help, so what do you say? Are you ready?"

The Shoebox Zoo exchanged glances, but Hunter's rousing words had done their job. "We're ready!" they cried, their whoops and cheers echoing around the empty corridor.

Marnie and Kyle crouched behind the swing door, waiting nervously until the footsteps had trudged past. They didn't pass. Instead, they slowed, paused and the

222

door swooshed open.

It was Becky. "What are you doing here?" she said slowly.

"Hi," said Marnie cautiously. And even though her thoughts were buzzing with the task ahead, she couldn't help noticing that all was not well. Becky's feisty, mischievous air had gone, leaving a subdued, defeated girl in its place. Strangely, Marnie found that she missed the old Becky. "Are you OK?" she asked.

"Actually," Becky's face crumpled. "No, I'm not."

Marnie was taken aback by her bluntness.

"I don't know what's going on," said Becky, her bottom lip trembling. "My mom, this show, the whole thing has gone way too far... and I'm really, *really* scared."

"We can help," Kyle said urgently.

Marnie nodded, suddenly realising that it was true. They all wanted the same thing. "We can help you get your mom back – your *real* mom," she said. "But first, we need to get backstage."

Becky was silent for a moment, her eyes flicking between them suspiciously. "Look, I don't know what you're doing here," she said eventually, "and I'm not going with you, but I'll show you." She pushed open the door. "Come on."

CHAPTER TWENTY-SIX

BEYOND
THE BEYOND

I t was nearly time. The Dawn Queen emerged from her dressing room at Channel 411, her face calm, but utterly determined. Toledo trailed miserably in her wake, holding the hem of her white cloak off the ground, like a reluctant, overgrown – and not terribly pretty – bridesmaid.

"This is the day," said the new star of *Above and Beyond the Beyond*. "This is the hour."

As they approached the studio, a rhythmic chanting noise began – barely noticeable at first, when the studio door magically swung open, it could be heard in all its deafening glory. "*Dawn Queen! Dawn Queen! Dawn Queen!*" The Dawn Queen smiled appreciatively.

Marnie and Kyle watched from backstage.

"Look at her…" said Kyle. "We haven't got a chance!"

But it was the sight of another that had left Marnie feeling like she'd been pummelled by a baseball bat. The last time she'd seen him, the last time she thought she'd *ever* see him, he'd been engulfed by flame. There stood Juan Roberto Montoya de Toledo – Michael Scot's incarnation of pure evil, who had killed his creator. Could she ever hope to defeat him and the monster he had, in turn, created?

Anxiously, Marnie looked for the Shoebox Zoo, and froze. "They're gone!" she whispered. "We can't do this without them!"

"Ahem," said a tiny voice. "As official spokesman for the Shoebox Zoo, may I simply say how pleased we are to be part of such a truly heroic—"

Marnie grinned with relief at the assembled animals. "No time for speeches, Eddie!" she said.

Nearby, the hands of an ancient white clock clicked round a notch and, simultaneously, the *On Air* light glowed red. The audience hushed as Toledo strolled towards the centre of the stage, where two bright circles of light illuminated *The Book of Forbidden Knowledge* – still revolving on its turntable – and the heap of cash.

"Ladies and gentlemen," he said. "The amazing, the mystical, the marvellous… the *Dawn Queen!*"

The audience erupted into a frenzy of noisy excitement, abruptly silenced by the appearance of a spectral figure that seemed to float in the semi-darkness. Suddenly, the woman threw back her head to reveal

225

her terrible face – the deathly white skin, glowing eyes and tiny, black pupils – and the rest of the lights snapped on.

In a rasping, inhuman voice, the Dawn Queen addressed her studio audience and the millions watching at home. "*I have come!*" she roared. "Your greed and stupidity have brought me!"

Momentarily, the audience looked stunned. Then the *Applause* sign flamed red and they clapped and cheered enthusiastically. Whether they'd been hyped up, hypnotised or were simply blinded by the promise of riches, Marnie couldn't tell. But she did know that powerful magic was at work here.

"You have invited me into your happy homes," the Dawn Queen continued, speaking viciously into the nearest television camera, "so I can feed on your ignorance and superstition and grow fat and bloated on the vapid dullness of your imagination!" With every word, her tone grew louder and more depraved, until she was screaming with rage.

Automatically, the studio audience cheered, but it seemed that the Dawn Queen had lost patience with them now. She thrust out her palms and fired torrents of white energy towards the prize money. It turned to dust. There were scattered cheers from the audience as the Dawn Queen directed the crackling energy towards them. Then there was silence. Little piles of white dust were all that remained of the poor, deluded audience.

Watching from home, Gramps, Grandma and Marnie's dad jumped. Then – *fzzzt!* – they all jumped again as the television screen went blank, the lights went out and the room was plunged into darkness.

"Oh, great," said Gramps.

Back at the studio, Toledo prepared for his starring role in the proceedings. "And now," he announced to the camera lens, "I believe it is time to open *The Book of Forbidden Knowledge!*" He reached his slender fingers towards the slowly spinning tome.

Marnie took a deep breath. It was now or never. "No!" she shouted, stepping from backstage, almost buckling in the face of the deadly duo's combined wrath. But, in one hand, she clutched the Bow of Wisdom, and in the other, the Arrow of Truth. She was ready to do battle. "You shall *not* open *The Book of Forbidden Knowledge!*" she bellowed. "It is the wisdom and the folly of the great Michael Scot, *and you will not have it!*"

The Dawn Queen whirled to face her. "The vainglorious Michael Scot is dead," she said icily. "Who will prevent me now?" Her upper lip curled into a sneer. "*You?*"

"*We* will!"

Marnie looked back gratefully as Kyle stepped forward. "Hurry!" he whispered to her. "Time's almost up." It was true. The hands of the ancient clock were rapidly approaching the number eleven.

Backstage, the four Shoebox Zoo creatures gripped

227

each other tightly – paw to wing and tail to paw. Sparks began to crackle between them. And, as the Book spun to a grinding halt, something magical happened. In the air, a metal eagle, a stone bear, a golden snake and a blue-and-gold wolf appeared – one above each corner. Glittering threads of light linked them together.

Marnie closed her eyes and concentrated all her thought, all her energy, all her power to make the magic happen. And it did. The four objects from Nathaniel's medicine bag materialised above the Shoebox Zoo creatures – the bear-claw necklace, the snake rattle, the eagle feather and the wolf tail. As the hands of the clock ticked nearer and nearer to eleven, more sparkling strands shot between the floating creatures and antiquities, until all eight were joined by a grid of glittering gold.

The clock struck. *Bong!*

The Book of Forbidden Knowledge glowed with a light so brilliant that it was unspeakably beautiful. At that precise moment, a fifth creature appeared high in the air, galloping for all he was worth. Yet more magical strands appeared, and somehow, as he ran, Hunter seemed to be holding everyone and every-thing together.

Bong!

She had been silent for so long, that Marnie had almost forgotten she was there, but suddenly, the Dawn Queen roared into life. "*Bows and arrows?*" she shrieked. "*Claws and feathers*? Do you think that the power of science and magic can be swayed by such barbaric trinkets?"

Bong!

In reply, Marnie placed the Arrow of Truth into the Bow of Wisdom and carefully took aim.

Bong!

The Dawn Queen ran to the Book, reaching towards it, clamping eager fingers onto its shining cover, only to be hurled back across the studio by an unseen force. She let out a cry of fury, while Toledo, watching from a safe distance, simply laughed.

Bong!

The Book of Forbidden Knowledge was in Marnie's sights. She pulled back the bow string, ready to fire—

Bong!

"Wait!" shouted Kyle urgently. "There's something missing!" He was staring at a point high above the Book. "Can't you see it?" he said. "The Falls of Faith!"

Bong!

Marnie followed his gaze, but all she could see was the velvet backdrop to the studio set.

Bong!

"You've got to trust me!" shouted Kyle. "Fire from the Falls of Faith!"

Bong!

For a moment, Marnie felt torn. But then she knew what to do. She closed her eyes and focussed, watching as…

…*Chief Stone Bear shot the Arrow of Truth from the Falls of Faith*…

…and when the vision cleared, she found herself perched on the edge of a cliff, looking down into the gushing torrent of water that she remembered so well – the Falls of Faith.

Bong!

"Hurry!" Kyle's voice echoed all around.

Bong!

Marnie looked down into the rushing water and saw the Book falling over the Falls. She took aim and fired.

Bong! The clock struck for the eleventh time.

All this time, Toledo had hung back – watching, waiting, looking for his chance. And as eleventh chime died away, he dived towards the Book, grabbing it with both hands. Triumphantly, he held it aloft. "At last!" he cried. "It is mine!"

Meanwhile, Marnie's arrow shot through the Falls and into the Channel 411 complex, down one corridor, up the next, through a set of swing doors, and towards Toledo. *THWACK!* The Arrow of Truth pierced *The Book of Forbidden Knowledge*, embedding itself deeply in the pages that Michael Scot had filled so long ago.

Waves of blinding, crackling energy flowed out of the Book, until Toledo was utterly consumed, and the Dawn Queen's face contorted, white-hot evil spilling from her eyes. She screamed in pain, collapsing to the floor, where she lay dazed and breathless. But she was changed. The Dawn Queen had gone, and in her place was…

"Mom!" Becky cried with relief, running from backstage to where her mother lay. The hippy, scruffy, slightly wacky Aurora Dexter was back.

Marnie and Kyle hugged with relief.

And so, the Quest was completed, the Book was destroyed, and *Above and Beyond the Beyond* was axed after only one, memorable episode.

Marnie went back to Scotland at the end of the school holidays, but she and her father – and the Shoebox Zoo – made a special trip back to the States to celebrate her twelfth birthday, on the eleventh day of the eleventh month.

It was a *great* party.

But there was something else Marnie had to do while she was in town…

The dog-eared, battered old shoebox held tightly in her arms, Marnie walked slowly towards the junk shop. She stepped inside and the door closed behind her, muffling the sounds of the noisy Denver street.

Junk was strewn everywhere. There were cracked ornaments, badly drawn pictures, tattered books. It was a wonder anyone ever bought anything at all. Marnie thought back to the bizarre place in Edinburgh where she'd found the Shoebox Zoo – the two shops were so like each other and yet so different.

Taking a deep breath, she opened the lid. Edwin, Ailsa, Bruno and Wolfgang stared up at her, already in tears.

"But *why*?" sobbed Edwin, brushing a tear away with his good wing.

"You guys sacrificed everything so that the Book would be destroyed," she said gently. "You sacrificed your only chance to be human. And that sacrifice was so special – you're all so special – that one person can't hold onto you. I can't be the only Chosen One. There are plenty of other kids out there who need your help…" Her voice broke, as she thought how the Shoebox Zoo had been with her during the most difficult year of her life, when she'd learnt to cope with her grief.

"We'll miss you," Wolfgang said bravely.

Marnie nodded tearfully. "Edwin… Ailsa… Bruno… Wolfgang…" She looked at each of them in turn. "You're like my mom. You'll always be in my heart. For ever. I promise." And before she could change her mind, Marnie whispered, "Back to sleep." Instantly, they froze, becoming the lifeless toys they'd been when she'd first met them. It seemed like a long time ago. Reluctantly, and for the very last time, she closed the lid.

"Anybody home?" she called. Her voice echoed eerily, but no one came. So Marnie McBride placed

232

the shoebox on a dusty counter. "Take care," she murmured sadly, before slowly turning and walking away.

The door clanged shut and the junk shop became very quiet. The only movement was dust floating through the patches of dim sunlight. Then there were footsteps. A shadow fell over the shoebox and a hand lifted the lid. One by one, Edwin, Bruno, Ailsa and Wolfgang opened their eyes and looked up hopefully.

"What do we do now, master?" asked Edwin.

THE END